I0623150

BAIT AND SWITCH

ST. CLAIR FAMILY SERIES

BOOK THREE

.

ERIN STEVENSON

Happy Jack Publishing

Copyright © January 2019
by Erin Stevenson Quint

Cover Design by Tina Lampe

ISBN: 1-944104-25-9
ISBN-13: 978-1-944104-25-2

PROLOGUE

DANE

DANE CORSICA PUT the car in park, turned the engine off, and stuck the key in the pocket of his leather jacket. Then he tipped his head back, closed his eyes, and got into character.

Thirty seconds later, he exited the vehicle and strode confidently into the waterfront seafood restaurant. He knew exactly where he was going, and passed the check-in station where about a dozen people were waiting to be seated. No one gave him a second look. Dane walked through the restaurant to a door in the back that led to a private dining room.

He slipped through it and took in the scene. Ten people, all of whom he expected. Except for one.

Oh no, what is she doing here? Dane's eyes bored into hers, and she stared back, never blinking.

"All right, now that pretty boy is here, we can get started," grumbled the man at the head of the table.

I'll deal with you later, Dane telegraphed to the woman.
Bring it, Corsica, she telegraphed back.

REAGAN

REAGAN ST. CLAIR slipped into a chair on the back row and adjusted her designer sunglasses on the bridge of her nose. Good. No one noticed her late arrival.

She smoothed the full skirt of her flowered halter sundress over her knees. The dress, high wedge sandals, and the luxurious blond curls flowing from under her oversized couture summer hat were so far from her usual look that surely, no one would recognize her.

Reagan's right leg began to tremble. She clasped her hands tightly together and pressed them against her knee, willing the shaking to stop.

I hate weddings.

The image of Paul in bed with her best friend still had the power to sear Reagan's memory, even ten years later. His and Reagan's wedding was just a month away, and everything had to be canceled, despite his pleading and begging for exoneration.

Reagan could forgive, but not for infidelity.

Her gaze drifted over the small bridal party gathered in front of a rose-covered arch and rested on her brother Landon, standing as best man for their younger brother, Brandon. The St. Clair men cut fine figures in their tuxedos. Standing at six foot four, they could pass for twins even though they were almost a year apart in age. Their features were nearly identical, the only difference being that Landon was blond and Brandon's hair was dark brown.

There looked to be less than a hundred people gathered for the small, intimate Sunday afternoon wedding. From the back, Reagan recognized a few older relatives that she hadn't seen in years. She supposed the others in attendance were from the bride's family, or some of her and Brandon's colleagues.

"Join hands, please," the minister said. Brandon turned to face his bride, Morgan, and the look of pure love and joy on her brother's face nearly broke through Reagan's façade. If anyone deserved happiness, it was Brandon. His first wife of over a decade, Darla, had been tragically killed in an automobile accident two years ago. Reagan hadn't met Brandon's bride yet, and hoped she didn't have to today.

Two little blond girls in pink and lavender flowered dresses stood with them. They had to be Brandon's daughters, April and Shelbie. Reagan had seen them only once, at their mother's funeral. She recalled the maelstrom of emotions she felt when meeting them for the first time: incredible sadness for their loss, an unexpected overwhelming connection with them upon the realization that they were her flesh and blood, and a complete lack of knowledge of how to interact with such small children.

The early afternoon sun beat down on the garden wedding, and Reagan was happy for her ridiculous hat. She craned her neck to get a better view. Morgan was similar in coloring to Darla, but tall and slender. Morgan and Brandon had met exactly a year ago on Mother's Day at a family event, yet another one Reagan had missed.

She would have missed this family event, too, if she didn't need a place to hide. After this current mess with her job was over, Reagan was going to do some serious soul searching and figure out how to reconnect with her family.

Her leg began to tremble again, and before she could reach for it, a man slipped into the seat next to her. He wrapped his hand around hers and squeezed.

Dane. Her unlikely comrade-in-arms, given their respective careers. Always there for her. Reagan let out a breath and squeezed back.

"Breathe, Reagan," he whispered in her ear. "We'll get through this."

2

DANE

DANE CORSICA SLIPPED a casual arm around Reagan's bare, tanned shoulder and took the opportunity to glance behind them. He did a sweep one way and then the other. An outdoor wedding was a logistical nightmare from a security vantage point. Too many ways in and out. But Dane was convinced they hadn't been followed.

He smiled to himself as one of Reagan's blond curls brushed against his fingers. Who knew she could be so gorgeous? Dane had known her for four years and had never seen her in a dress, or any makeup save a dash of lip gloss. The absence of Reagan St. Clair's signature long, dark brunette braid was the most dramatic change of all.

It was a good disguise, one that might save her life.

Dane resisted the urge to yawn. They'd been on the run for almost seventy-two hours, and needed to get completely underground. Dane didn't know who he could trust.

But Reagan did.

When she'd pitched her idea for them to come to the Chicago area for this family wedding, Dane was completely against it. Despite that Reagan was distant from her family, she insisted that she still wanted to be part of this day and see her brother get married. And since they had to get out of Florida and go *somewhere*, why not go to Illinois?

He'd finally relented, and told her it would work for the short term. But then, he would have to find a better solution, a deep, off-grid place to keep both of them safe while he unraveled this mess. The problem was, he couldn't go to any of his usual sources. Reagan insisted that her brother, Landon, could find something for them.

Dane had never seen Reagan so certain, so resolute, and he was out of options. So here they were, mere feet away from someone Dane had never met, but whom he would have to trust to keep both himself and Reagan alive and safe.

It went against everything the DEA had taught Dane, but he trusted Reagan, and Reagan trusted her brother. That would have to be good enough for now.

"I now pronounce you man and wife," the minister announced. He smiled at the groom. "Brandon, you may kiss your bride." Dane came out of agent mode just long enough to witness the bridal couple's loving embrace. He looked away.

"Ladies and gentlemen, I'm proud to introduce, for the first time, Dr. Brandon and Dr. Morgan St. Clair!" *That's right, Reagan said he's an MD and she has a PhD.* The audience broke into applause.

Dane tightened his arm around Reagan. "You ready?" He felt her nod. "It's up to you now."

3

REAGAN

REAGAN KNEW SHE would have just a split second to catch Landon's attention. *Please, God, let him remember.* Then she winced inwardly. It was highly unlikely that the Almighty would listen to her. They hadn't been on good terms in years.

Reagan had placed herself on the aisle so that she would have the best chance of making eye contact with her brother. She watched her nieces skip by, hand-in-hand. Then came their father and new mother, their faces bursting with joy. Brandon didn't even look her way. If Reagan had been holding up a flashing neon sign announcing her presence, she doubted he would have noticed.

Here we go. Next came Landon with the matron of honor, his dark-haired wife, Kelsea, who was also Morgan's sister. That's how Brandon and Morgan had met. Reagan lifted a hand to touch the brim of her hat, and the movement caught her brother's eye.

The instant his eyes connected with hers, Reagan moved her hand an inch and tugged on her right earlobe.

Score. Landon's amber eyes widened for a split second, but he didn't break stride, and he and Kelsea were gone.

Reagan casually turned to Dane. "He saw me," she murmured.

"Good job," he whispered. He looked around. "Let's get out of here before any of the other guests start coming by." That was fine with Reagan. She didn't want to chance seeing her parents or her sister. Not until this case was closed and she was safe again.

They rose, and Dane took her hand, pulling her behind a row of tall bushes. "There's an unlocked shed about fifty yards to the south," he said. "Down a slight slope and around behind some trees. You're sure your brother will know to follow us there?"

Reagan nodded. "Positive. He'll be watching me. Our old signal meant *trouble, meet me right away.*" It was from long ago when she and her brothers had fancied themselves amateur detectives in their Wisconsin hometown, but Dane didn't need to know that.

"Well, if anyone else notices us slipping away, they'll just think I want to be alone with the most beautiful woman here." Dane winked at her.

"In your dreams, Corsica," Reagan smirked. In all the years that she and Dane had worked together, he'd never crossed the line, probably because Reagan had never given him any encouragement. He was handsome, to be sure, and the best agent—DEA, FBI, or otherwise—that Reagan had ever worked with. But he was also nine years younger than her (he thought it was only seven since Reagan had fudged about her age), and that was too much. It just didn't feel right to her. Sometimes when she made a pop culture reference from her era, Dane would look at her blankly.

Despite that, he was incredibly mature for his age, and one of the best friends Reagan had ever had. But sometimes, when you tried to make it something more, the friendship didn't survive. And Reagan needed all the friends she could get.

The reception was set up on the deck behind Brandon and Morgan's cedar home on a rolling country property west of Chicago. It was a beautiful setting. From their vantage point behind the bushes, Reagan watched the crowd making its way up to the deck. She thought she recognized a couple of her cousins. Then her heart gave a lurch as she saw her parents, each holding the hand of a small girl and boy. Those must be Landon and Kelsea's twins. She swallowed. *More next-generation St. Clairs.* She felt a familiar twinge of regret that she would probably never give her parents grandchildren. Then followed the ever-present justification that given her time-consuming career and discomfort around children, it was probably for the best.

"Dear heaven, who is *that?*" Dane hissed into her ear. Reagan followed his eye to a petite young woman in a flowered sundress, with thick, honey-blond hair that cascaded halfway down her back. She had sparkling brown eyes, dimples, and a thousand-watt smile. As she greeted someone, her melodious laugh floated to them on the breeze.

"That's my sister, Sara." Sara looked even more grown-up than she had just a few months ago at Christmas.

"She's a little taller than you, but other than that, she could be your twin," Dane murmured. His eyes were riveted on Sara. "Your *much* younger twin," he added.

Reagan bumped her shoulder against his arm. "Gee, thanks," she drawled. But he was right. It hadn't occurred to her, but she and Sara looked very much alike except for their hair color. Now that Reagan was disguised as a blonde, the resemblance was a bit eerie. "She's, um, fifteen years younger than me."

Dane frowned at her. "Really?" *Oops. He's probably trying to do the math.*

Reagan nodded. "She was mom and dad's surprise. The boys were twelve and thirteen when Sara was born. They've always called her *Peanut*."

Dane and Reagan began to stroll toward a line of trees, and the ground got a little more uneven. Dane put his hand around Reagan's waist to steady her. "I don't want you to fall off those shoes," he said drily.

Reagan resisted the urge to laugh. "Thanks. These sure aren't my Birkenstocks," she retorted. She picked her way gingerly around a tree root.

She saw the wooden shed in the distance, and in another twenty seconds or so, they reached it. Dane pulled the door open and ushered her in, then pulled the door almost closed, leaving a sliver of an opening.

Reagan's eyes adjusted to the dark, and she took off her sunglasses and her hat, and set them on a short stack of wooden crates. Dust motes danced in the sunlight streaming in from a west-facing window. The shed contained a riding lawn mower, wheelbarrow, and the usual yard implements. "This isn't so bad."

"Well, I should be able to scope out a good hiding place," Dane said with a smile. He didn't say anything, and seemed to be perusing her. "I don't think I've ever seen you in a dress."

Reagan let out a breath and fingered her skirt. "Yeah, it's been a while." She thought for a moment. "Maybe the South Florida Press Awards banquet, three years ago?"

"Yeah, I wasn't there," Dane said with a laugh. "You look completely different without your braid."

"Don't I know it?" Reagan said. Without it, she felt like she was missing a friend.

There was a soft tap at the door, and Dane sprang in front of her, his hand moving quickly inside his jacket. He turned his head and put a finger to his lips.

"Reagan?" came the whisper through the crack in the door. Dane nodded.

"Yes, come in," she said softly. Dane took a step to the side. The door opened, and Landon entered. He reached for Reagan, and she saw Dane pull the door closed behind him.

"Oh my gosh, Reagan." Landon's arms came around her, strong and secure. Reagan felt rare tears coming to her eyes. "What are you doing here? You haven't been answering any of our texts or calls, so I figured you were chasing a story." He pulled back and looked at her. "What's with the hair?" He fingered a curl and smiled. "You look like Peanut."

"I know," Reagan replied. She couldn't go soft now. Dane materialized at her side, and Reagan cleared her throat. "Landon, this is Dane Corsica." The two men shook hands. "Dane's DEA."

Landon didn't blink. He looked at Dane. "You armed?"

Dane pulled one side of his jacket back to reveal his holster.

Landon nodded, and looked back to Reagan. "What's going on?"

Reagan exchanged a glance with Dane. She pulled a

dollar bill out of her purse and held it out to her brother. "I want to hire you as my attorney."

Landon tilted his head at her. He pocketed the bill and looked between her and Dane, his features serious. "Okay, anything you tell me is now protected by attorney-client privilege."

Reagan let out a breath. "Well, the short story is that I work with the DEA sometimes on news stories, and Dane and I trade favors." Landon's eyes darkened a shade.

"Not those kind of favors," Dane muttered. Reagan's face burned.

"Reporters and agents have mutually beneficial relationships," she explained.

Landon rolled his eyes. "Yeah, that sounds a lot better, sis. Go on," he prodded.

Reagan was aware of Dane standing next to her. Why was she flustered? "So anyway, Dane has been working a case undercover, and I got an anonymous tip and went in undercover to investigate on my own, and we ended up at a meeting together, in Miami. It's a drug case connected to Cuba."

Landon frowned. "Sounds like just another day in South Florida." Dane smirked.

"Right," Reagan said. "So anyway, Dane and I ended up at this meeting, and neither of us knew the other one was going to be there. We left separately, and arranged to meet up at one of our normal drop spots where we leave information for each other. But one of us was followed, and we were shot at."

"What?" Landon asked sharply. "Were you hit?"

Dane shook his head. "We managed to get away, but we

don't know which one of us was followed, or by whom. Reagan—"

Landon put his hand up. "Hold it." He turned his palm up.

"Oh, got it," Dane said, and produced a dollar bill. Landon slid it in his pocket. "Go on."

Dane nodded. "We've shared our information, but it doesn't sync up, and we need more time to figure it out. This story has the potential to be really big. I snuck home and got a few things that I needed to go underground, and planned to finish making the arrangements the next day. But Friday morning, it was all over the news in Miami that the two of us were being sought for questioning about this drug case. I think somebody turned on us."

Reagan picked up the thread. "We needed to get out of Florida, and I really wanted to come to Brandon's wedding, so I convinced Dane to come here."

Dane put his hands on his hips. "I have a private network that I use in situations like this, to find safe houses or get cash or weapons to me, but obviously I can't trust anyone." He paused. "I'm not willing to chance it. So we're completely on our own."

Landon palmed the back of his neck and looked at his sister. He let out a breath. "You always had to be Nancy Drew," he muttered. A smile tugged at the corner of his lips.

Reagan rolled her eyes and tried not to laugh. "He and Brandon were the Hardy Boys," she said to Dane, "but they grew up to be a lawyer and a doctor instead."

Landon looked at his sister with pride. "And you grew up to be the best investigative reporter to ever work for the *Miami Herald*."

Reagan frowned. "Well, I'm an Assistant Editor now, but you know reporting is in my blood. Anyway, I was trying to wrap this up so I could come to Chicago, but I wasn't sure I could, so that's why I wasn't answering any of your texts or calls. When Dane and I realized we needed to get out of Florida, I insisted that we come here. To *you*," she added.

"Landon, can you find somewhere we can hide?"

4

DANE

DANE SAT DOWN next to Reagan on the bed. They were in a spare bedroom in the basement of Brandon and Morgan's home. Landon had snuck them a plate of food, two pieces of wedding cake, and some punch.

"Is it spiked?" Reagan asked hopefully. Landon shook his head.

He was gone now, and Dane and Reagan were alone. She removed her hat and shoes, and sat on the bed rubbing her feet.

"How do women stand these?" she groaned. "Shoe designers must be in cahoots with podiatrists and chiropractors."

Dane pushed her hands aside. "You're about to be treated to the Dane Corsica magic fingers foot massage," he announced, wiggling his fingers.

Reagan yawned. "If I wasn't so tired, I'd argue with you." She lay down on her back and smoothed out her skirt. "All right, Corsica. Work your magic."

Dane stood and removed his suit jacket, unbuttoned his sleeves and pushed them up, then resumed his spot next to her and started rubbing. He didn't know a thing about how to give a foot massage, but he wasn't about to let her know that.

"I like Landon," he said. "I can see now why you wanted to come to him for help. The attorney-client privilege thing was a good idea." Dane could tell that Landon was still a little wary of him, but that was a good sign, too. After they'd told Landon everything, he said he needed to get back to the reception, and also needed a few moments to think about next steps.

So Dane and Reagan stayed in the shed and fifteen minutes later, Landon returned and gave them instructions to go through an unlocked walkout basement door and then to the bedroom and wait for him there.

Dane rubbed Reagan's feet for a little while longer and they chatted.

"Should I start calling you *Nancy*?" He couldn't resist teasing her.

"We were such dorks," she said with a laugh. "The three of us were convinced we were helping to keep the streets safe for the citizens of Baraboo, Wisconsin."

Dane laughed. "Baraboo? You're making that up."

"It's real. Check the map."

"Is it anywhere near Green Bay?"

"Nope. It's closer to the Dells." She smiled. "That's one redeeming quality about you, Corsica." He and Reagan shared a deep devotion to the Packers.

They fell silent for several minutes. "Do you think he'll be able to find us a place to hide?" Dane asked. He was already trying to figure out his next move if Landon St. Clair didn't come through.

Reagan didn't reply. She had dozed off. *Maybe I have the magic touch after all.*

It was going to be interesting, going completely off-grid with Reagan. Dane took the opportunity to stare at her heart-shaped face. She really was lovely with makeup and wearing a blond wig and a dress. This Reagan was very different from the real Reagan. That Reagan wore jeans or cargo shorts year-round, plain t-shirts, flip-flops or Birkenstocks, little to no makeup, and of course, her dark brunette braid.

The real Reagan St. Clair moved comfortably in the still-male-dominated world of newspapers, was amazingly tech-savvy, and one of the smartest women Dane had ever met. She was small and spare, but Dane had seen her go toe-to-toe with men twice her size, and reduce them to rubble.

She could also drink most of them under the table, and he'd seen her use that to her advantage.

Dane looked at his watch and yawned.

A knock sounded at the door. Reagan sat up and Dane's hand automatically went to the grip of his weapon. "It's me," Landon's voice came. He poked his head in. "I have Kelsea, Brandon, and Morgan with me," he said.

Dane and Reagan looked at one another for a couple of seconds.

"That's the deal," Landon said. "You can trust them. Everyone else has left."

"Mom and Dad and Sara?" Reagan asked. "And all the children?"

"Yes," Landon said.

Dane nodded, and Reagan followed his lead. She started

to run a hand through her hair as though to tidy it, then realized the futility of it and stopped. "Okay," she said.

"But we meet here. We stay in this room," Dane said. Even though they were surrounded by people that Reagan trusted, Dane was still vigilant. He had reconnoitered the basement, and knew two ways to get out.

Landon opened the door, and in came the two women, still in their wedding finery, and Brandon in his tux, minus the jacket, who immediately went to Reagan and scooped her up in his arms. "You came," he whispered. "Thank you."

Dane saw that Reagan was fighting for composure, unusual for her. He stood and extended his hand. "Dane Corsica," he said. "Congratulations." He shook Brandon's hand and nodded to his new wife.

Morgan stepped forward and enveloped Reagan in a hug. "Thank you for coming. It means so much to Bran."

"Welcome to the family," Reagan said politely.

Kelsea St. Clair followed suit. "I'm so happy to see you again, Reagan," she said. Dane knew Reagan well enough and wondered why her brothers hadn't told their wives that she wasn't really a hugger.

There was a moment of awkward silence, and Dane and Reagan sat on the bed again. Brandon St. Clair lowered himself onto the only chair in the room and pulled his bride down to sit on his knee. Landon moved a small ottoman over for his wife. "Kelsea's expecting again," he said proudly.

Reagan didn't say anything. "Congratulations," Dane offered.

"It's another set of twins," Kelsea said. She rolled her eyes in her husband's direction. "He walks in the house, and I get pregnant with twins."

Everyone laughed, and it broke the tension.

"Is that how it works?" Brandon said with amusement. He looked at Landon. "Bro, I think you and I need to have a talk. There's a better way to achieve that." Everyone laughed again, and Dane decided right then and there that he really liked Reagan's brothers.

When the silence settled in, Landon took the lead. "I've given them a very broad sketch of your situation," he said to Dane and Reagan. He looked at the three newcomers. "Do you have any questions?"

Morgan St. Clair gestured to Dane's holster. "Is that loaded?"

"Yes, it is. Believe me, Mrs. St. Clair, we're all safer with it loaded than not."

She blushed and looked at her husband, then back to Dane. "I love being called Mrs. St. Clair, but you can call me Morgan."

Brandon gave his wife a squeeze, and his expression was so full of love and adoration that Dane had to look away.

The newly-married groom looked at his sister. "Landon said you were being Nancy Drew again," he said with a wink.

Reagan rolled her eyes. "Why did I come here?" she muttered.

"Seriously, Reagan, what were you doing?" Brandon asked.

Dane wanted to take charge, and stood, assuming "agent" stance, shoulders back, feet firmly planted, thumbs hooked on his belt loops. Still, Landon towered over him by a few inches. "Reagan and I were both working undercover on a case. One of us was followed, and we were shot at. Now the authorities are looking for us." He looked somberly at Brandon and the women. "This has the potential to be really big, but I don't want to share any of the details beyond what Reagan has told her attorney." He glanced at Landon.

"So, what are you going to do now?" Brandon asked.

"Reagan's safety is my only concern," Dane said. "I have this weapon and another one with me, and several thousand dollars in cash. I bought a car with cash, but I want to get rid of it soon. That's how we got here. I have other assets stashed in places around Florida that I would normally go to, but law enforcement is looking for both of us down there. We had to flee."

He looked at Reagan, and her normally proud and confident posture had vanished. Her arms were wrapped around her middle and she appeared smaller than she was. Dane lowered himself down next to her, and she immediately sat taller. He looked at Landon. "I won't leave her. I can't trust any of my usual resources. We need a place to stay, completely off grid." He turned to Brandon and Morgan. "Don't worry, we're not asking to stay here," he said. "It's not secure enough."

Dane thought that Brandon looked a little relieved. Morgan certainly did.

Kelsea St. Clair looked at her husband. "What about—" She flipped her gaze to Dane and Reagan. "Would you consider going out of the country?"

Landon nodded. "I was thinking the same thing," he murmured.

Dane rammed a hand through his hair. "I would, but I don't have an alias for her, no passport or documents. That's the one thing I didn't get to before the bottom dropped out,"

he said. "And I only have one set of documents for myself."
It had all happened too fast. He looked at Landon. "Where
were you thinking?"

"St. Jardin."

Dane nodded. "Interesting." He knew of the picturesque
island country, but had never been there. "Do you know
someone there?"

Landon and Kelsea exchanged an amused look. "We sure
do," Landon said. "Our close family friends own a honeymoon
resort on St. Jardin. That's where Kelsea and I met."

It took a moment for those words to sink in. *Isn't
everyone at a honeymoon resort already married?* But Dane
had to let that go for now. "It sounds great, but without a
passport, I can't get Reagan there." He racked his brain. "It's
too big a risk for me to use any of my regular contacts to get
documents made."

The six of them sat silent for several moments, deep in
thought.

"Peanut!" Brandon exclaimed. Everyone looked at him
quizzically.

"Oh, I get it," Landon said. He looked at Reagan. "We use
Sara's passport for you." His eyebrows lifted. "It might work."

"Other than the fact that posing as someone else and
using their passport is probably a federal offense," Kelsea
commented.

Landon's face showed no emotion. "There are
loopholes."

"What about the age difference?" Dane asked. He was
still figuring that out. Either Sara St. Clair was younger than
she looked, or Reagan was lying about her age.

"Hey!" Reagan said with a frown.

Dane looked at her. "I'm not trying to be funny. It's a legitimate concern," he said apologetically.

"Maybe if you were questioned about it, you could say that 'Sara' has been ill," Brandon suggested.

No one said anything. Dane stood and crossed his arms in front of him. "What about your friends who own the resort? Can we leave them out of the loop on this? I really want to contain this to the people in this room."

Landon stroked his chin. "Rose and Ike Goldman. They're an older couple," he said. He looked at Kelsea. "I know they can be trusted, but yes, I think it's best to not share the details with them. You want to blend in and be treated like all the other couples there." Everyone nodded.

"Their honeymoon package runs from Sunday to the next Saturday." Landon looked between his sister and Dane. "Can you two pose as a newlywed couple for the next week?"

Dane's eyes met Reagan's. Her expression didn't change one iota. The classic Reagan St. Clair poker face. "Yes," they said in unison.

Landon nodded. "You'll be missing the first day, and you don't have a reservation, so I'll have to call the Goldmans and set that up."

"You could tell them that you have friends whose honeymoon plans—uh," Dane stopped, trying to think of his next words.

Kelsea St. Clair's brown eyes lit up. "Whose honeymoon plans fell through. They discovered at the last minute that it was a scam."

Landon and Dane nodded. "That works," Landon said. "So you'll be Sara and—whatever your alias is, a newlywed couple. That way, her passport can still say St. Clair."

"Ike and Rose haven't met Sara, have they?" Morgan asked.

"No," Landon said. He looked at Reagan. "Just make sure the Goldmans never see your passport. Rosie is sharp. She knows how young Sara is and would see through the 'illness' story in a heartbeat. Always use your married name—your *fake* married name." He turned to Dane. "What's your alias?"

"Trey Armstrong," Dane replied.

Landon nodded. "That works."

The group sat in silence for another moment. "I'm waiting for someone to poke another hole in this," Dane said.

The silence continued.

"Duh," Brandon said. "How do we get Peanut to give up her passport?" He looked to his brother. "We can't bring her into this. She can't keep a secret."

"I'll handle her," Landon said. No one else said anything.

"She isn't planning any international travel for the next few months?" Dane asked.

"No, she's nannying for us," Brandon said. "At least she has been, but now that we're married, Sara's going to go back to Wisconsin to Mom and Dad's." He looked at his bride. "But, we're—" he squeezed her hand and grinned. "We're adopting a baby boy. We're picking him up on Wednesday in Indianapolis."

Dane immediately slid a glance at Reagan, and her façade cracked ever so slightly. "Oh— congratulations," she sputtered. She quickly regained her composure. "That would be a great excuse to get Sara to stay a little longer, wouldn't it?" she asked.

Landon looked at his brother and new sister-in-law. "If you

guys would do that, I'd feel better having the real Sara under our control, so to speak. At least to know her movements."

Morgan nodded. "I'd welcome the help, actually. She's terrific with the girls."

"Good, that's settled," Landon said. "And just so we're clear, we're not bringing Mom and Dad into this in any way, until absolutely necessary. Hopefully after everything is wrapped up and Reagan is safe and there's no story to tell." He looked at his sister.

"That's more than fine by me," Reagan said.

"When can we leave for St. Jardin?" Dane asked. "I want to get out of Chicago. Someone's going to figure out quickly that Reagan has family here, and come sniffing around."

"Are we in any danger?" Morgan St. Clair asked.

"Not so long as you claim that you haven't seen Reagan recently." Dane sighed. "I wish I could order a protection detail for all of you, but my hands are tied."

Landon appeared to be calculating. "I think we can fly you out tomorrow night. I'll get you a hotel room tonight with cash, and tomorrow we can get you both outfitted to go on a tropical honeymoon."

"I volunteer to shop," Kelsea St. Clair said brightly. Her husband, Morgan, and Brandon laughed.

Landon looked around the group. "Anything else?" His gaze rested on Dane.

"I'll need you to pick up some things for me, too. Electronics and such," Dane said.

"I can do that." He eyed the group one more time. "All right, that's a wrap," Landon said. Everyone stood. "Sis, I know you may not be into praying these days, but I want to pray right now." Dane could tell it wasn't a request.

He saw Reagan swallow. Landon held a hand out to Reagan, and to Kelsea on his other side. Reagan grasped Dane's hand, and Dane found himself holding Morgan's hand. The circle closed, and they bowed their heads while Landon prayed for Dane and Reagan's safety, God's blessing on their plan, and Brandon and Morgan's new marriage and family.

Dane hadn't been part of anything like this for a long time. He pushed those memories aside. Despite his discomfort, peace settled over him like a warm blanket. Yes, this was strange, indeed.

5

SUNDAY EVENING

SARA

SARA ST. CLAIR closed her eyes and breathed in the scent of roses and gardenias. She'd caught the bridal bouquet that her new sister-in-law, Morgan, had thrown. It wasn't even a contest. You would have thought Morgan had eyes in the back of her head, her aim was so true.

Sara gently laid the bouquet on the dresser and sat on the bed. It had been a beautiful wedding and a nearly perfect day with family. The only thing that made it less than perfect was that their older sister, Reagan, hadn't shown. Because of their age difference, Sara and Reagan weren't really close, but why would her sister not show up for Brandon's wedding? She hadn't even returned phone calls or texts. Sara knew that Brandon had held out hope that Reagan would swoop in at the last minute. Sara tamped down a frisson of irritation. No doubt her sister was tied up with some big news story. With Reagan, work always came first.

Now, Brandon and Morgan were sequestered at their

home for two blissful days alone. The rest of the family was camped out at a Chicago area hotel with an indoor water park. Jim and Janice St. Clair, Landon, Kelsea, and hers and Morgan's mom, Beth, were armed and ready to pamper and spoil all the grandkids. Sara was there, too, but her parents had gotten a separate room for her and told her to relax. She'd been taking care of April and Shelbie for almost a year and although she adored them, it would be nice to have down time.

What to do with an entire evening to herself? She'd stuffed herself with the delicious food at the reception, so she wasn't hungry. Maybe she'd go to a movie. But first things first, to get out of this dress.

As soon as Sara had changed into jeans and a comfortable top, there was a knock at the door. She smiled to herself. *I wonder if Grandma and Grandpa need reinforcements already.*

She opened it and saw that it was Landon.

He frowned. "That was quick. Did you look through the peephole? I didn't hear the chain disengage. Did you even have it on?"

Sara rolled her eyes as he brushed past her into the room. The door closed behind him. "No, and no. Who else besides the family would knock at my door?"

He turned to face her, hands on hips. "You're too trusting, Peanut."

"Landon! I am not a baby," she countered. "I spent most of the last year completely in charge of your nieces. Brandon trusted me. I'm almost twenty-two years old. I'm an adult." She planted her hands on her hips, mirroring his pose. "If it was midnight, the chain would have been on, and I would have looked. It's five thirty."

He squeezed the bridge of his nose with one hand, and dropped the other one to his side. "I know, Pea—Sara, I'm sorry," he murmured. Landon let out a gusty sigh. Sara was surprised to see genuine contrition in his amber eyes.

"Look, can we sit? I need to talk with you about something."

"All of a sudden, you're all serious," Sara said, eyeing him warily.

Landon lowered himself into one of the chairs, and Sara sat down across from him on the bed. "Yes, I have a serious, adult-sized problem that I need your help with," he said. "And right now, you're the key to solving it, but the thing is, I'm not going to be able to explain much. You're going to want answers, but you'll just have to trust me."

Sara was intrigued, but didn't say anything for a few seconds. She couldn't imagine her oldest brother having a problem only she could solve. "Okay," she responded quietly.

"I need to borrow your passport." Landon said the words evenly, and his gaze was steady.

"My—my passport?" Sara was thoroughly confused. Her passport had exactly one stamp in it, from her history class trip to England her senior year of high school. And it had sat in her desk drawer ever since. Why would her brother want her passport?

"Yes." He continued to look at her steadily.

"I—wow. That's an unusual request," Sara said, fishing for a little more information.

"It is." He wasn't biting.

She twisted her lips as her mind whirred. "It must be important."

"It is."

Sara let out a sigh of frustration. "Could you just tell me—"

Landon interrupted her. "The only thing I can tell you is that it might save someone's life."

Sara lifted her eyebrows. "Oh." She was silent for a moment. "How long do you need it?"

He lifted one shoulder. "Not sure. A week or two at most." He paused. "Are you planning to leave the country?"

"Well, no." The passport was just sitting in her desk drawer collecting dust. Sara knew her brother wouldn't ask this of her unless it was really important, and it sounded as if it was.

"All right, then." Landon leaned forward, elbows on knees. "I need it as quick as you can get it. Best case scenario, you leave right now, drive home, and bring it back tonight."

Goodness. "Tonight?" Sara watched in amazement as he reached in his pocket and produced a set of car keys. She gasped with delight. "You're letting me take your new car?" Kelsea and the twins had flown to Chicago earlier in the week and rented a vehicle. Landon drove his own up from St. Louis on Friday.

Landon grinned and lifted the keys up high before Sara could grab them. "It's mine, but the firm leases it." Landon was a partner at St. Louis' most prestigious law firm, originally Jacoby & Jamison. They rebranded themselves as JJS when they named Landon a partner several years ago and had since grown into a widely respected and revered legal powerhouse.

Sara popped up and lunged for the keys, and Landon stood. She got her hands around them, but he held on. "I mean it, Peanut, set the cruise control. No speeding. No food in the car. You can have a drink, but it has to have a lid."

Sara rolled her eyes. "When did you turn into Dad?" she muttered. He released the keys into her hand.

"What were you planning to do tonight?" he asked.

"Nothing, really. Maybe go to a movie."

"Do you have friends from college who live around here?"

Sara considered that. "Yeah, not real close friends, but a few other people. Why?"

Landon stretched and let out a yawn. "That'll be our story. I don't want Mom and Dad to know about this. If it comes up, you met up with some friends to hang out."

Sara busied herself transferring things from her small clutch that she carried to the wedding back into her regular purse. "Whatever, that works."

"And no calls or texts to anyone about going home tonight, or about this—at all."

Sara began to open her mouth. "Not even Caitlyn," Landon said quickly.

Not even her best friend? She stopped and looked at him. "This feels like a cover-up, big brother. This—whatever you're doing—it's legal, right?"

Landon gave her a stern look. "You know I can't break the law," he said. Then he relaxed his expression. "But I can twist and bend it a bit. You let me worry about that. Just go home, grab the passport, and get back here. Text me when you're on your way back."

Sara nodded, and headed for the door. Landon was right behind her. He reached down to give her a hug. "Thanks for doing this, Sara. I know you're all grown up, but you'll always be our Peanut."

SUNDAY EVENING

REAGAN

DANE AND REAGAN'S flight left O'Hare almost an hour late and bumped all the way to Atlanta. After a short layover, the flight to St. Jardin was much smoother, for which Reagan was thankful. Shortly after takeoff, she pretended to fall asleep. Reagan needed some time to think. She was uncharacteristically rattled by her disguise, the fake marriage, and being with her family, even though she'd only made contact with her brothers.

It was wonderful to see both Landon and Brandon so happy and in love with their wives and children. Soon, they would have seven children between them! She wasn't at all jealous, but it magnified Reagan's failures and shortcomings in her own mind. She knew her parents were disappointed that she hadn't gone the marriage and family route. Reagan had no doubt that her younger sister would choose that path, even though Sara was "dabbling" in college and trying to figure what she wanted out of life. She was still so young.

After Paul's betrayal before their wedding, Reagan had thrown herself into her job to drown out the pain. Before she knew it, work completely filled her life. She loved what she did, and she was good at it, so it was just easier to take on more in order to build a higher, thicker wall around herself. She'd gone out with a handful of men over the years, but had a two-date rule. Only once had she thought about extending it to three, but decided in the end to stay true to herself.

And just like that, a decade had gone by and Reagan was, by her own devices, alone.

Reagan felt Dane shift in the seat next to her, and snuck a peek at him. He was either asleep, or pretending to be, too. He had to be exhausted. They'd spent almost twenty-four hours in the motel room that Landon got for them. Reagan had spent most of that time sleeping and Dane had spent most of it awake—making plans and dispatching Landon to purchase burner phones, a secure laptop, and all kinds of other equipment that Dane needed to conduct untraceable research on their case. Kelsea had gone shopping for all the personal items that Trey and Sara Armstrong would need for their honeymoon trip.

Reagan was now Sara Cecily Armstrong, even though "her" passport, of course, still had her last name listed as St. Clair. She glanced at Dane, who was beginning to stir. His papers listed him as Trey Michael Armstrong, from Traverse City, Michigan, which worked since the real Sara had been a student at the University of Michigan for two years. They'd made up a vague cover story about meeting there.

Dane touched her hand. *Make that Trey.* Reagan swallowed.

He spoke in hushed tones. "You like your rings?" His

finger moved over Reagan's wedding band and rested on the beautiful solitaire diamond.

"Well—I guess," Reagan stammered. "But I told you I didn't need the engagement ring. A plain band would have been fine." She stared at the gold band adorning Dane's finger. It looked so out of place.

"I know it would have been fine with *you*," he said, lowering his voice to a whisper, "but I was thinking about what Sara would want. You know—Sara with the blond curls and the dresses and make-up." Reagan didn't say anything, and Dane smiled. "That Sara would want a big, beautiful diamond, and since I'm expensing it and will be reimbursed for it in the long run, that's what I got—or rather, what Kelsea got."

Reagan smiled to herself recalling Kelsea's delight at being sent ring shopping. "You're right," she murmured, then sighed. It was beginning to annoy her, not being in her own skin. Not to mention that it was exhausting trying to act soft and feminine, two traits that most definitely did not describe her. But as Dane said when they set this up, the best disguise would be one that was as far from her real self as possible.

"Do you think you'll ever get married, for real?" Reagan asked.

Dane didn't say anything for several seconds. "I don't know," he finally said. "You?"

"I came close once," Reagan said.

"How close?"

"A month." She shrugged. "He cheated on me. I guess I'm glad I found out before the wedding."

Dane shook his head. "Don't settle. Hold out for the best.

The best of the best." He looked at her intently. "You deserve it, Reagan."

"Thanks," she said. "So do you."

"I enjoyed meeting your family," he said. "They're pretty religious." Reagan could tell it was just an observation; his voice held no censure.

"Yeah, they are," she said. "Just one more way that I'm different from them."

"You're not religious?"

"Not really. I was, you know, raised in the church and everything. Our family was there whenever the doors were open. But when I started getting interested in journalism my junior year of high school, it opened my eyes to all kinds of different world views. I started making new friends that didn't go to my church, and discovering new ways of thinking. It was so liberating."

Dane's eyes twinkled. "How liberating?"

Reagan slid him a smile. "No comment." She wanted to get the spotlight off of herself. "What about you? Do you go to church?"

Dane appeared to squirm. "Well—I was raised in a Christian family, too. But I kind of stopped going a few years ago, just got busy with work and—just other things."

"Well, you're in a high-pressure, high-stakes career," Reagan whispered, "and you're really good at what you do." Dane didn't reply, and that was typical of him. He didn't see how extraordinary an agent he was.

The plane started its final descent, and Reagan straightened in her seat. How long would they be stuck on this island, under the pretense of being married? Landon had told them that the usual stay at the resort was about a week.

What would they do after that if they still needed to stay underground?

She felt the landing gear come down, and looked out the window. It was night, and millions of stars glittered in the expanse above. Below, Reagan only saw darkness, and assumed that they were still over the water.

The plane touched down and bumped once before settling into its smooth coast down the runway. Reagan closed her eyes, pressed her spine into the seat back, and resisted the urge to extend her right leg and foot as if pressing on a brake pedal. She had flown all over the world on every kind of conveyance imaginable, and loved every aspect of flying except the landing. That probably stemmed from an incident on a transatlantic flight landing in Germany about seven years ago. It had been raining and for some unexplained reason that was never determined, the jet skidded off the runway. Luckily, there were no injuries, but it was still a very scary incident, one that Reagan hoped never to repeat. Her heartbeat sped up now, just remembering it.

She flinched and her eyes flew open when she felt Dane's arm come around her. "Relax, sweetheart," he murmured into her ear. "You can't jump every time I touch you if we're supposed to be married." His hand kneaded her arm.

"Dane—"

"Shh. Trey," he corrected her.

She swallowed. "Trey," she repeated. She lowered her voice to a whisper. "We need to set some ground rules about that."

One side of his lip twitched. "Don't worry, I promise

your virtue will remain intact," he whispered. His chocolate brown eyes sparkled.

"Just never mind about my virtue," Reagan whispered back. The jet was almost to the gate. "We'll talk about this later." She busied herself with her carry-on.

Dane removed his arm. "I look forward to it," he drawled with a dimpled smile.

DANE

DANE FOLLOWED HIS "wife" out of the terminal. Even though it was late night, the curb was filled with vehicles. Some of them even looked operational. He and Reagan had both traveled extensively in other countries and knew that sometimes, you had to take what was available, and pray that it got you to your destination in one piece. "What do you think?" he murmured.

Suddenly, someone grabbed him from behind, and Dane instinctively reached for his weapon. Which, of course, was back in Illinois with Reagan's brother.

He whipped his head around and let out a breath. There stood a slip of a girl with shining dark eyes and black hair pulled into a ponytail, holding a hand-lettered piece of cardboard that said *OOBER*.

"Hi! I am Monique! But you can call me Moni!" Her smile was nearly as wide as the island. "I drive. I take you anywhere you want to go," she said in a sing-song voice.

Dane resisted the urge to laugh. Moni looked like she

was about fourteen. "Hold on a minute." He looked at Reagan in the hope she would take charge.

Reagan eyed the girl and smiled. "You have a valid driver's license, Moni?"

Moni's head bobbed up and down. "Yes, I have driver's license. My Uncle Louie gave it to me."

Dane couldn't hold the laughter in this time. "How old are you, Moni?"

"I am seventeen," she said. Dane and Reagan exchanged a skeptical look. She held up her hand. "I never have accident, I swear. I will take good care of you and your lady." She reached out for Dane's roller bag. "I will drive slow and get you there safe."

Dane looked at Reagan. She lifted a shoulder. "Let's live a little, Trey," she murmured with a smile and a wink.

Dane held on to his bag. "I've got this, Moni. Just take us to the car."

Impossible though it seemed, her smile grew bigger. "You will be happy. I will keep you safe." She practically skipped along the sidewalk in front of them. They passed car after car, most of them dark, non-descript four-door sedans. Then Moni stopped, and extended her arms wide. "Ta-da!" she sang out.

"Oh, this is—your car?" Dane asked. She stood proudly in front of a rusted Gremlin that may have been lime green at one time.

"Yes, this is Sadie-belle!" Monique exclaimed. "My Uncle Louie gave her to me!"

Dane could tell that Reagan was having as much trouble holding it in as he was. He cleared his throat. "Uncle Louie is a generous guy."

"He won her in poker game!" Moni opened the trunk, which amounted to unhooking something that looked like an elastic hair tie wound between two hooks soldered to the trunk lid and bumper. "Sadie-belle is good car." After considerable pushing, pulling, and squeezing, they got the bulk of their luggage into the trunk and got the door mostly closed and secured with the hair tie. Dane and the rest of the bags ended up shoehorned into the backseat, with Reagan in the front passenger seat.

"Where to?" Moni asked, her ever-present smile dancing.

"Ah, the St. Jardin Honeymoon Resort, on Paradise Cove," Dane said.

Moni's dark eyes grew large. "Ah, Rosie and Ike! Ooh, la-la!" She exclaimed. "You newlyweds! I drive fast. I know you want to get there fast!" She popped the clutch and attempted to peel out from the curb, but Sadie-belle wasn't made to peel out. They came to a bone-jarring stop.

Dane felt his teeth rattle. "Moni, it's okay. We don't need to get there fast." *We just need to get there alive.*

A chorus of horns blared behind them. Moni leaned out her window. "Cool your jets, boys!" she shouted.

Dane covered his face with one hand and took a deep breath. *Maybe we should have taken our chances and stayed in Florida.*

The trip could have been filled with drama, but once they got out of the airport, Sadie-belle ran smoothly (for the most part) and Moni kept her original promise to drive safely (for the most part). She chattered throughout the entire thirty-minute trip about the island of her birth and her large, interconnected family, which of course included Uncle Louie, who ran a popular bar.

When they arrived at the resort and Dane peeled himself out of the backseat, he could hardly stand straight. Reagan noticed him rubbing his back, and busied herself getting everything out of the trunk while Dane pulled out his wallet. "How much?" he asked Moni.

She lowered her eyes and quoted a price that seemed ridiculously low to Dane. "Is that in euros or dollars?" he asked. "Never mind." He gave her twice what he thought she had asked for.

Her eyes grew wide as saucers, and she pumped Dane's hand. "Thank you, sir! You need anything while you are in St. Jardin, you go to the Bahama Llama Boogie Shack and ask for Louie." She poked a thumb at her chest. "Uncle Louie always know where to find me! Moni help you with *anything*!" She backed away, smiling and waving. "Thank you, sir! Thank you ma'am! You have good honeymoon! Ooh la la!"

As Sadie-belle lurched away, Dane felt a wave of exhaustion wash over him. All he could think of was getting a full night's sleep. Thanks to Landon, he had all the equipment he needed to dig into this case and get it solved. Then he and Reagan could get back to Miami and resume their lives.

Dane held the door open for Reagan and followed her into the deserted lobby. His gaze rested on the blond curls that hung halfway down her back, and the full, although rumpled, skirt of her blue and white sundress that swirled around her legs as she walked. He swallowed. *Our lives in Miami may look a whole lot different after this week.*

They stepped up to the desk and were greeted by a short blonde whose pink nametag read *Molli*.

"You must be Mr. and Mrs. Armstrong," she said with a friendly smile. "Welcome to St. Jardin! I hope you had a good trip."

"Yes, we are, and we did," Dane said. "Thank you." They quickly got through the check-in process, and were informed by Molli that breakfast would open on the patio at seven o'clock the next morning, and that the owners were looking forward to meeting them.

She handed them two key cards. "I'm sorry we don't have any bellhops on duty to help you with your luggage." Dane and Reagan assured her they would be fine.

As soon as they found their room and the door closed behind them, Reagan dumped her bags on the floor and turned to Dane. "Okay. Time for ground rules."

Dane held a finger to his lips, and took out a special piece of equipment about the size of a deck of cards. Reagan crossed her arms in front of her and waited impatiently until he had swept the room for listening devices. "All clear," he said.

"Ground rules."

Dane fought the urge to cringe. "Can we do this tomorrow? I'm exhausted. I just want to go to bed."

"Wrong choice of words, Corsica."

He rolled his eyes. "I meant *sleep*."

Reagan studied the king-sized bed, decked out in shades of pink. It had an abundance of pillows, which she grabbed and arranged in a wall down the middle of the bed.

"Really, Reagan?" He wasn't in the mood for one of her lectures.

"You'd prefer to sleep in the bathtub?"

He reached his arm out and snared one of the pillows. "At least give me one for my head."

She sighed. "Fine." She removed a pillow from the pile. "Don't take it personally, Dane. I share hotel rooms and beds with all kinds of colleagues when I'm on assignment. This is standard operating procedure."

"I guess I can—"

Reagan cut him off. "Rule number two: be fully dressed at all times, and anyone needing to change clothes does it in the bathroom. With the door closed."

"That sounds like two rules," Dane said. "So if we both need to change, we both go into the bathroom?" He couldn't resist adding a roguish smile. Engaging in this lighthearted banter was giving him a burst of energy.

She rolled her eyes. "You know what I mean."

"What's rule number three?"

"Rule number three is—stop it!"

"Stop what?" Dane asked innocently.

"Stop—looking so, you know—cute and silly." She look completely flustered.

"I can't help it if I'm cute, Reagan. It's my cross to bear." He rubbed his hands together. "Reagan St. Clair, rattled. The guys won't believe it."

"*The guys* will never hear about this," she countered.

"True." Still, it was fun to tease her. And she'd never believe him if he told her the reason why he had no designs on her.

Dane unzipped his suitcase, found his toilet kit, and headed for the bathroom. "In about thirty seconds, I'm going to be asleep on *my* side of the bed," he said firmly. "You can tell me rule number three tomorrow."

8

TUESDAY MORNING

SARA

SARA OPENED HER eyes and looked at the digital clock on the hotel nightstand. It was just after eight o'clock. Her parents had told her to relax and sleep in, but Sara still felt that she had to get up and get going. She still couldn't get used to it. *I don't have to be anywhere today. No classes, no job, no April and Shelbie to look after.*

Sara's quick trip home on Sunday night went off without a hitch, and she arrived back just after midnight and delivered her passport into Landon's waiting hands. He said he would cover for her Monday morning if she wanted to sleep in. Sara spent the rest of the day with the family, and especially enjoyed getting acquainted and playing with her youngest niece, Rose, and her little nephew, Isaac. Landon and Kelsea seemed to be busy with something and really weren't around much until late afternoon. After the little ones went to bed, the adults ordered pizza and played dominoes. It was a very relaxing day.

Sara flopped onto her side and pulled the light cotton blanket up. *Nothing to do today but figure out what to do with the rest of my life.*

When she had left college after her second year, dissatisfied with her major, the chance to take a break and nanny for Brandon's girls was an answer to prayer. All of her friends thought she was crazy to take on that kind of responsibility, and always asked how she could stand being with two preschoolers day in and day out.

But the fact was, Sara loved it. She had gotten the girls involved in all kinds of activities and made it a point to get to know their little friends and their nannies or au pairs, and in a few cases, their mothers. Sometimes, she offered to watch the other children, and had a blast playing with them and coming up with all kinds of fun things for them to do. It honestly didn't bother her to have charge of half a dozen little ones all at once.

Now, she was actually entertaining the idea of going back to school for an early childhood degree. Education was a big deal in her family, and Sara was expected to complete college, and she wanted to, even though she hadn't landed on the right major yet. But in the meantime, she needed to decide whether to go back to Chicago with Brandon and his growing family. Immediately after the wedding on Sunday, when he and Morgan had made the joyous announcement to the family about the baby, they begged her to come back and help with April and Shelbie for another few weeks or months while they got settled. Sara didn't know what she was going to do in the fall, so she might as well go back to Chicago. She would need to make a decision pretty soon about school. It wasn't as if she could show up on the first day of classes.

Just as she was going into the bathroom, her phone rang. It was her best friend, Caitlyn. They'd met the first day of choir freshman year, been inseparable throughout high school, then gone to the University of Michigan together to major in vocal performance. The difference was, Caitlyn knew exactly what she wanted to do and was now just a year away from obtaining her degree.

"Hi, Boo," Sara said into the phone. She set it on speaker and laid it on the counter.

"Hey, Boo," Caitlyn answered back. They had called each other this for so long that neither of them could remember how or why it began.

"How was the wedding?"

"Oh, it was gorgeous, perfect. I'm so happy for Brandon and Morgan. And guess what? They're adopting a baby boy this week—he just fell into their laps. It was one of those God things." She explained more of the details.

"Did you catch the bouquet?" Caitlyn asked.

Sara snorted. "Yes. *That* was a waste. I'm not even seeing anyone."

"You never know," Caitlyn said. "So, when will you be home?"

"Tomorrow. I know you were hoping we could spend the summer together at home, but I'm probably headed back to Chicago next week to help out with the girls while they get settled with the baby. I don't know how long I'll be there."

"Boo! You can't!" Caitlyn wailed.

"I'm sorry," Sara said. "I'll miss being with you, too."

"That's not it," Caitlyn explained. "You're not going to believe what I have to tell you."

"What?" Sara said. She got her toothbrush out, rolled paste onto it, and started brushing her teeth.

"I just got a phone call from one of the Disney producers down in Florida," Caitlyn said. Last summer she'd gotten a job singing at Disney World. Sara had auditioned and been accepted too, but gave it up to help Brandon's family. "They had a last-minute cancellation and need a soprano. I turned it down—you know, because I'm taking summer school so I can graduate next spring. But I told him you might be available, and he pulled your audition tape and wants to talk to you!" Caitlyn let out a squeal.

Sara dropped her toothbrush into the sink and did a quick rinse. "You're kidding me!" She looked at her astonished reflection in the mirror, then turned and went back into the bedroom. Her mind was swirling with the implications of this door opening. Was this God's way of pointing her in a direction? The second chance to sing with Disney was huge. But what about Brandon and Morgan and their family?

Sara sat down on the bed. "Oh, wow. I have no idea what to do." She pulled her thick blond waves into a ponytail.

"You're going to call Lance Petrie back right now!" Caitlyn exclaimed. "He's waiting to hear from you. I'll text you his number. You *have* to do this, Boo, you'll never get another chance."

Sara's heart skittered. "I know. Okay, I need to think about this. But I'll call him. Thanks." She disconnected and within seconds, got Caitlyn's text with the phone number. She stared at it, and thought about Brandon and his family. Sara had already come to his aid once. Why did they still need help? Most families got along fine when a new baby joined the family, unless the mother needed extra time to recover from the birth, which certainly wasn't the case now.

"I'm doing this for me," Sara whispered. "God can still close this door if this isn't the path He wants for me." She said a quick prayer, and made the call. Her heart pounded as the phone began to ring.

"Lance Petrie," came the deep voice.

"Oh, hi—hello, Mr. Petrie," Sara said, willing herself to calm down. "This is Sara St. Clair, calling from Wisconsin. You—"

"Sara, yes. Hello! It's great to hear from you. Please, call me Lance."

"Okay, um, Lance. Well, I hear you have an opening for a soprano."

"No, we have an opening for *you,* Sara. I was in another part of the organization last year, and didn't hear your tape until now. You're fantastic. Why didn't you sing with us last year?"

Sara's heart began to beat erratically. *Wow.* "I—I had a family situation come up. I was needed—well, I was just needed." She didn't want to get into a bunch of details.

Lance spoke quickly but sincerely. "I admire that. But I hope the family can get along without you this year. When can you be in Orlando?"

This was moving fast! Sara's mind raced. She would need to get a hold of Brandon, and talk with her parents. She took a deep breath. "When do you need me?"

"Day after tomorrow? We're already in rehearsals. We'll make your flight arrangements. We'll e-mail you a list of everything you need to bring. Oh—you have a passport, right?"

Sara's heart plummeted. "Um, well, yes, sure, but won't I just be in Orlando?"

"Nope," Lance said. "This show is going to do some Caribbean island hopping from the get-go, so you'll need your passport. I need to run, Sara. My assistant will e-mail everything to you, you'll need to sign and fax or e-mail the contract back to us, and if you have any questions, just ask her. I'll probably meet you in a couple of days. I'm so happy you're going to be with us this year!"

"Thanks, Lance," Sara managed to say. Her mind was reeling. No way was she letting this opportunity slip through her fingers. *How am I going to get my passport back?* She had no idea what Landon planned to do with it, just that he'd have it back to her in a couple of weeks.

But now, she'd been handed the opportunity of a lifetime, and Sara didn't have a couple of weeks.

She got up and paced back and forth, then called Landon's cell, which went straight to voicemail. Maybe he and his family were sleeping in, although with twin toddlers, she doubted it. Sara nibbled at her thumbnail. She hated to bother Brandon on his honeymoon, but she needed answers and something told her that he would know what was going on. Her brothers were super close and had no secrets. Sara was going to have to let Brandon know that she wasn't coming back to Chicago, but wasn't ready to do that yet, until she could solve this passport issue.

He picked up on the third ring. "Hey, Peanut." He sounded completely relaxed, which made Sara feel guilty for letting him down.

"Hey," she said. "How are the newlyweds?"

"Very happy," Brandon said. Sara loved hearing the deep contentment in his voice. "So what's up?"

"Right," Sara said. "Well, I was wondering if you knew anything about why Landon asked to borrow my passport."

Brandon didn't respond for a moment. "What did he tell you?"

"He didn't tell me anything. Just said it was a personal issue and to trust him."

"And you trust him, right? So you gave it to him."

"How do you know I gave it to him?"

"I don't. I was asking if you did." Brandon said, but Sara knew she had caught him.

"You weren't asking, you were *telling* me that you knew I gave it."

"Peanut, you're splitting hairs. Why are you asking about this now?"

"I just started thinking that it was a really strange request, and wanted to know." She waited a few seconds. "You know something, don't you, Brandon?" Sara was confident she could squeeze the information out of him. She'd had years of practice, and she knew her brothers. There was a reason why Landon was the attorney in the family, and Brandon wasn't.

"Look, I—" Brandon let out a breath. "Landon is the one who made the request. He should be the one to share the details, if he wants to."

"I tried to call him, but his phone was off." Sara didn't admit she could just walk down the hall and ask him in person, but she'd have to concoct a way to get him alone. "Come on, Brandon, you owe me." She inserted levity into her voice so he'd know that she wasn't upset with him. "I put my life on hold for you."

He laughed. "Oh, you're going to keep bringing that up forever, aren't you?"

"If necessary," she said with a smile. "Come on. I don't need *all* the details. Just tell me a general idea. I'm intrigued." The fastest way to get information out of Brandon was to pretend that it wasn't important.

He sighed loudly. "Okay. It was for Reagan."

"Reagan?" Sara couldn't imagine. *Landon said my passport could save someone's life! Was he talking about our sister?*

"She got herself in some hot water working on a story and needed a place to hide. Landon sent her to the honeymoon resort on St. Jardin to hide out for a little while. She disguised herself as a blonde, and since she looks like you—well, do I need to spell it out?"

What? Where and when did they see Reagan? Sara sat down on her bed in disbelief. Reagan had traveled to St. Jardin on Sara's passport? Was that even legal? It had to be, if Landon had arranged it. "Are you kidding me, Brandon? When did you see Reagan?"

She heard her brother gulp. "Sara—it's not important."

"It's important to me! You haven't been out of Chicago in over a week. Was she here, in Chicago?"

Brandon didn't say anything, and Sara decided to wait him out. Finally, he spoke. "We saw her, just after the wedding. She was there."

Sara gasped. "Where? I didn't see her."

"They came late and sat in the back row, and left right away, and didn't stay for the reception."

"I can't believe this. Did the whole family see her, except for me?"

"No, not Mom and Dad. Just Landon, Kelsea, Morgan, and me."

It all made sense now, Landon's request for the passport. "So you guys just left me out. I'm so tired of being treated like a child!" Tears pricked at her eyes.

"Pea—Sara, I'm sorry. We just didn't—it all happened very quickly, and Landon thought this was the best way to handle it."

Sara couldn't wait to get off the phone and give it to Landon with both barrels. But then she changed her mind. *They left me out of their plan, so I won't include them in mine. I'll figure out a way to get my passport back on my own.*

But she couldn't let anything on. She took a breath and sighed. "I overreacted, I'm sorry."

"It's okay, Peanut."

Sara rolled her eyes to herself. *Things will never change.* "Well, I have to go. Hug Morgan for me."

"If I have to," Brandon said dramatically.

Sara disconnected and tossed her phone down, then flopped back on her bed and rubbed her forehead. *What am I going to do?* She lay there for several minutes until a plan begin to form in her mind. *Can I really do this? YES, I can. I'm almost twenty-two years old, I'm an adult. If I drag my brothers into this, they'll put up all kinds of roadblocks. I'll always be "Peanut" to them, but I'm a grown woman and can make my own decisions.*

She ticked through the points in her plan just to make sure she'd covered all the bases. Sara had driven her own car down from Wisconsin, so that wasn't a problem. She'd spend a little time with the family today and tell them about the last-minute invitation to work with Disney—leaving out the part about needing a passport. Then she'd drive home, pack for the summer, and implement the rest of her plan. And she would call Brandon.

Sara sat up and grabbed her phone. There was the text from Lance Petrie's assistant, Dawn. She punched in the phone number. "Hello, Dawn? This is Sara St. Clair. Could you please make an adjustment to my flight to Florida? I need to fly into Miami tomorrow, first thing. I'll get myself up to Orlando the day after. Thanks for your help."

REAGAN

REAGAN LOOKED AT herself in the full-length mirror and tugged at her white shorts. They were shorter and tighter than she was used to. She had paired them with a bright orange sleeveless shirt made out of some soft, flimsy material that had a ruffle along the v-neck. She hated the ruffle, but all of the other clothing items in her suitcase had something just as objectionable.

The bathroom door opened, and Dane came out, looking rested and chic and casual in Bermuda shorts, a form-fitting blue t-shirt, and topsiders.

He gave a low whistle, and Reagan wished the ground could swallow her up. "Look at you, Mrs. Armstrong," he said, showing his even, white teeth.

Reagan slipped her feet into flat, comfortable sandals. Dane—"

"Trey," he corrected her. "Come on, get with the program, Sara," he said in a teasing voice. He stepped closer, and Reagan caught a whiff of his aftershave.

She rolled her eyes. "This shirt is awful." She began to unbutton it. "I'm going to change." Then she noticed Dane's raised eyebrows and felt herself flush. Her hands stilled.

"You almost broke rule number two!" Dane exclaimed with mock horror. "I was going to tell you not to change, but on second thought, go right ahead." He grinned at her.

"Whatever!" Reagan was flustered. "At least you're wearing clothes that match your normal style." She quickly did up the buttons. "I haven't worn a ruffle since I was— like, five."

"You look great. Come on, we're already late for breakfast."

"Let me check my hair one more time." Reagan's hair was now dyed blond, thanks to a connection Morgan had sent to the hotel before they left Chicago, an elite hairstylist with some kind of special, fast-acting hair dye. Dane had decided that with the abundance of water activities on the island, it would be safer than a wig. Reagan stepped in front of the mirror and made an adjustment. "I wish I could have just slapped it in a braid," she muttered.

Dane laughed. "I'll bet you do. Come on, let's go. I'm hungry."

"You're always hungry," Reagan grumbled. She leaned closer to the mirror. "I think I put on too much mascara." She let out a frustrated sigh. "I barely know how to do all this stuff. Kelsea gave me a crash course."

"She's a nice gal," Dane commented. "Both of your sisters-in-law seem great."

"They are. My brothers chose well." Reagan wished she could get to know them better, but felt completely inadequate when she thought about how they had it all—fabulous husbands, motherhood, and their respective careers. Kelsea owned a thriving pet sitting business, which she ran from home with a crew of teenaged employees, and Morgan was an artist and college professor.

"All right, I'm ready," Reagan said. Dane held the door for her. As soon as it closed and locked behind them, Reagan gasped. "Oh no, I forgot my key card!"

Dane slipped his hand in his pocket and flipped a key card out. It quickly disappeared again. "Good thing I'm here to take care of you."

"Oh, that'll be the day, Cor—" Reagan was startled as Dane swooped in and kissed her on the cheek, near her mouth.

"You can't call me *Corsica* out here," he whispered in her ear. "And loosen up." He put his arm around her waist, and started walking. "Good morning," he said pleasantly to a couple who was approaching from the other direction.

Reagan pasted a smile on her face and nodded at the couple. This was going to be a long week. As soon as they were past, she turned to Dane. "You just broke rule number three! No kissing."

"It was only on the cheek," he whispered. He took her hand. "*Sara,* we can't be convincing to anyone if you act like the ice queen."

"I am not an ice queen! And you're *not* here to take care of me." Nothing got her hackles up more than a man telling her that she needed to be taken care of.

Dane looked at her in frustration. "All right, simmer down." He turned to face her, gently squeezed her arms, and looked around. "You have my word, I won't break any of your rules." His voice got even quieter, and his eyes were serious. "We're good friends, and I don't have any intention of altering that." He was silent for a beat. "Understand?"

Reagan nodded. "I just don't feel like myself. I feel completely out of control."

"You're not *out* of control, but you're not *in* control, and you're not used to that." He raised his eyebrows at her. "Am I right?"

Reagan literally felt a weight come off her shoulders. "Wow, yes, you're right." Dane took hold of both of her hands.

"I need to be in control now," he said. He looked around and lowered his voice. "I know you don't like that, but we're still on an assignment."

Reagan let out a breath and nodded. "Okay," she said reluctantly. Dane let go of her hands and offered his arm, and they walked in silence.

They arrived at a beautiful patio behind the main lodge, overlooking the turquoise sea. The breakfast buffet was loaded with all kinds of delicious-looking food. "Landon and Kelsea warned me about this," Reagan whispered to Dane. "I'm sure gonna want to run every day, or I won't be able to fit into anything by the end of the week." She stopped with a spoonful of cheesy hash browns mid-air. "Hey, maybe that's a thought."

Dane laughed. "Did you bring your running shoes?"

"Oh, shoot! No. Maybe I could buy some in town. Kelsea told me they have shopping expeditions."

They walked to a table in a far corner with their plates and sat down. Dane made sure to sit facing the patio, and lowered his voice. "I'm not sure we should leave the resort. And we're not flush with cash right now, either."

Reagan frowned. "Landon offered to loan you some money."

Dane cut into his waffles and took a hearty bite. "I know," he said as he chewed. "But I already had to accept a loan from him for some of the equipment. And this isn't a vacation, remember that. Please," he added with a smile.

Reagan nodded, and popped a red, ripe strawberry into her mouth. It was probably the best one she'd ever tasted in her life. She reached for another one.

A woman's voice cut into her thoughts. "Hi! We're Drew and Cassi Carson, from Pierre, South Dakota. May we sit with you?"

Dane and Reagan exchanged a glance. "Sure," Dane nodded with a smile. Reagan forced a smile, too.

The Carsons sat. "Where are you from?" Cassi chirped, her strawberry-blond curls danced. Her fair-haired husband smiled and nodded at them.

"We're Trey and Sara Armstrong, from Michigan. Nice to meet you," Dane responded politely.

"Hello," Reagan murmured.

"Your hair is beautiful," Cassi gushed to Reagan. "Is it natural?"

"Honey!" Drew Carson shook his head and looked at Dane and Reagan apologetically. "Sometimes, she has no filter."

"I'm just being friendly," Cassi said with a smile. Apparently, her husband's apology didn't faze her. "Have you ever been to the Caribbean? This is our first time." She seemed to have quickly lost interest in Reagan's hair.

"No, we've never been here," Reagan said.

"We just got married last weekend." Cassi rubbed her

husband's shoulder. "This is so exciting. Did you just get married, too?"

"A couple of weeks ago," Dane said. "On the—" It looked to Reagan like he was trying to figure out the date.

"On the second," she said, coming to his rescue. "May second."

"Yes, that's right, May second," Dane said.

"You'd better remember your anniversary, Trey. Get it tattooed somewhere to remind you," Drew Carson said, which elicited a laugh from everyone. Reagan didn't recall seeing any tattoos on Dane and wouldn't, unless he broke rule number two, or maybe if they went swimming.

"Good morning!" Reagan looked up to see a spry, white-haired couple approaching. From Landon and Kelsea's description, she knew it had to be Rose and Ike Goldman. She had shared about them with Dane, so he was prepared, too.

"You must be the Armstrongs," Rose said. She was pink from head to toe, from her pink-tinged bouffant hair to her pink Converse, her trademark. Her pink rhinestone cat-glasses glittered in the morning sun.

Dane stood to shake their hands. "Yes, I'm Trey, and this is my wife, Sara," he said, touching Reagan's shoulder. She greeted the Goldmans and kept her head down. Landon and Kelsea had cautioned her about getting too close to Rose. The woman had never met Reagan or her sister, but she'd seen family pictures. Even though they were a few years old, Kelsea said if anyone were to make the fantastical leap from young Sara to present-day Reagan as a blonde, it would be Rose.

"We're so glad you could salvage your honeymoon," Rose said.

"Oh no! What happened?" Cassi Carson's blue eyes filled with concern.

"There was a mix-up with our other plans, and they fell through," Dane said. He looked at Rose and Ike. "We really appreciate you letting us come a day late."

"That's no problem, son," Ike said, patting him on the arm. He exchanged a look with his wife. "We're especially happy to help friends of Landon and Kelsea St. Clair." Reagan buried her nose in her cup of yogurt.

"And we want all of our couples to get the best start to their marriages!" Rose said.

Cassi giggled and laid her head on Drew's shoulder. "I can't imagine being anywhere better than this!" she exclaimed. She looked at Reagan. "Just wait until you see the sunset tonight!"

To Reagan's relief, Rose and Ike moved on to the next table after a kind offer to come find them if they needed anything. She dug into her breakfast again, and Dane did the same, while Cassi chattered and Drew mostly listened and nodded.

The Carsons finally left with a promise from Cassi to find them at lunch and sit together again, and Reagan let out a breath. "That's the worst part about being at one of these places, when someone like that gloms into you and wants to hang out all the time."

"Yeah, and no room service here," Dane said, "so we have to come out of the room for meals. Man, that was good," he said, rubbing his stomach. "Landon warned me."

"Do you want to go for a walk?" Reagan asked.

Dane frowned. "No, sorry, we need to get back to the room." He lowered his voice to a whisper. "Remember, we're not on vacation." He stood and held out a hand to Reagan.

"And no one will question us if we just stay there." He wiggled his eyebrows and Reagan felt her face heating up.

When they got back to their room, Dane locked the door behind them and retrieved his laptop and other equipment from his suitcase that was inside the closet. Reagan swept the room for bugs and gave him a thumbs-up.

They sat down together at the table. Dane rubbed his hands together. "Okay," he said, "Let's get started. I feel ready to tackle this after a good night's sleep."

Reagan folded her hands in front of her. "Squeak is the key to this. I feel it in my bones."

Squeak was the nickname used by just about everyone in Florida for their popular governor, who had been a high-profile state politician for over three decades. Dane threw his head back and let out a gust of air. He and Reagan had had this discussion in the car on their way to Chicago. "Reagan, you can't solve cases by feeling something in your bones."

"Are you telling me you never trust your instincts?"

"Yes, but I never let them lead me. You have to let the *facts* lead you." Reagan started to interrupt him, but he had a head of steam going. "Fact: our squeaky-clean governor has been in public life for over thirty years without one blemish on his record. You've met him. He's the cleanest guy—well, he's the cleanest guy I've ever seen. A public servant, completely upright, terrific family, not one whiff of any trouble with any of them."

She nodded. "Yes, I've met him on several occasions, and you're right. He's the epitome of clean. But people can change, Dane. You've seen how the lure of drug money can tempt the cleanest of them."

"Where's your proof? You saw the governor talking with

Doug Navarro at a public gathering." This is what had brought Reagan to the meeting back in Miami.

She tilted her head at him. "Dane, it wasn't a smile and a handshake at a public event. I took a shortcut behind the stage to get to someone on the other side, and the two of them had their heads together in a secluded spot behind the stage. Navarro is one of the drug cartels' dirtiest operatives. Can you think of one reason that our governor would be anywhere around him?"

Dane shook his head. "Reagan, take a step back—"

His tone sounded placating, and that made her mad. Reagan raised her voice over his. "You know how the governor prides himself on being completely transparent and above-board. Every pie that Navarro has his fingers in is questionable at best. He has dozens of lowlifes to do his dirty work, and insulates himself. That's why you, the FBI, and even the Miami cops have never been able to hang anything on him. There's *nothing* good about Navarro. There's no reason for Squeak to be in his presence, let alone having a serious discussion with him."

"I know, I know, you told me," Dane muttered. "Okay, let's review *my* case from the top. Navarro has been making a lot of trips back and forth to Cuba since some of the trade restrictions between the Cuban government and the US are starting to lift. He's representing a conglomerate of businessmen, and it looks like just another cocaine smuggling operation to the DEA. There's a pattern to those, but over the past couple of months, that pattern has changed, but we don't know why. That's why I was sent in undercover. And then you showed up at the meeting and everything fell apart." Dane rubbed his eyes.

Reagan crossed her arms in front of her chest. "You act like it's my fault that everything fell apart."

"That's not what I meant. I was just stating the sequence of events. You showed up at the meeting. Everything fell apart."

"And we still don't know what any of this has to do with our governor," Reagan said.

Dane corrected her. "We still don't know IF any of this has to do with our governor. Reagan, it just doesn't make any sense."

Reagan crossed her arms in front of her. "He's the key to this, I'm sure of it."

10

DANE

DANE WAS GLAD they weren't required to dress for dinner. To him, *dressing up* meant wearing shoes instead of sandals. He was a Florida native and enjoyed the casual culture. Dane wore a suit when he had to, but felt much more comfortable in the clothes he now wore: a blue and white striped button-down shirt, untucked and open at the neck, khaki shorts, and his topsiders.

What was taking Reagan so long? Dane rapped on the bathroom door. "Can we go? I'm getting hungry."

"Do you have a tapeworm or something, Corsica?" Reagan snapped. "I'll be out in a minute."

He squeezed the bridge of his nose. *Gosh, she sure is prickly today.* Dane thought back to his and Reagan's earlier conversation. He didn't want to reveal that he'd known the governor personally most of his life, having been a long-time friend of Dane's dad. Reagan had some good points, but Dane couldn't reconcile them with what he knew of the man.

Reagan marched out of the bathroom, looking lovely in a peach and yellow sundress and matching sandals. Her hair was piled on top of her head and parts of it sort of stuck out, but it was pretty, and he told her so.

She grunted. "I can't stand this long hair in the heat. If I can't put it in a braid, this messy bun thing is the next best thing. Kelsea showed me how to do it."

Dane resisted the urge to sigh. *All I did was give her a compliment.* "You could put it in a braid if you want," Dane said. "It's blond. It's not going to give you away."

Reagan shook her head. "I don't think I should. Having it *not* in a braid helps me to stay in character."

They arrived at the main dining room and stood in line with other couples. When they got to the front, they were told that each couple would dine alone tonight, and to choose one of the small, round tables. Dane took Reagan's hand and led her to one in the farthest corner, and pulled out her chair.

She looked as if she might protest, then clamped her lips together. "Thank you," she murmured as she sat. Dane took his seat with his back to the wall.

"Good girl," Dane whispered. "See, it's not so hard."

A server came and offered them drink choices. They both ordered the non-alcoholic fruit punch.

Dane waited until the server was out of earshot. "You could have had a drink."

She shrugged. "I know, but I would have felt funny drinking if you weren't. And I know you don't."

Dane was surprised she'd noticed. "You do? When did you figure that out?"

She laughed. "I've known you for four years. So I figured it out about three years, eleven and a half months ago."

Dane frowned. "We haven't spent that much time together outside of work."

"Call it my reporter's nose." The server delivered their drinks and left. Reagan took a sip. "Oh, this is really good. I don't even miss the alcohol."

Dane smiled. "I have a question for you. Landon and Kelsea met here, at this honeymoon resort, but if they weren't married, why were they here?"

"That's a funny story," she replied. "They were both supposed to marry other people on New Year's Day. Kelsea's fiancé backed out a few days before, and Landon— well, he was literally left standing at the altar."

"Ouch."

"In front of five hundred people. It was awful."

"I'll bet," Dane said.

"Both of them had made a reservation here for their honeymoons, and they both decided to come alone. So Rose pretty much threw them together."

Dane laughed. "She's something else."

"And then, on the last night, all the couples had to take part in this historic island ritual, some kind of symbolic marriage ceremony—but it wasn't legally binding—and a couple of weeks after they got home, Landon and Kelsea found out that they really were married."

Dane's eyes opened wide in amazement. The server set salads down in front of them. "There's more to the story," Reagan said. "It's much better coming from them. You'll have to ask them to tell you about it sometime," Reagan said.

An uneasy feeling settled over Dane. "Do you think we'll have to do that symbolic marriage ceremony?"

Reagan's fork stopped in mid-air. "Gosh, I don't know.

I didn't even think about it. We'll have to figure out a way to get out of it." She shrugged. "I can come down with a migraine or something."

Dane nodded and took another bite of his salad. There was no way that he was going through any kind of a marriage ceremony. *No way.* If Reagan's "headache" didn't do the trick, Dane would think up something else to get them out of it, even if he had to shoot himself in the foot.

Then he remembered, his weapon was back in the states with his other possessions that Landon now had.

"That was amazing," Reagan said. "I may never eat again. Until breakfast!" she added with a laugh.

"I agree," Dane said. He stood and helped her to her feet. "Come on, let's get back to the room." He lowered his voice. "And hit the computer again."

Reagan came to a standstill and looked around. They were completely alone. "We've been cooped up in that room all day. We're at one of the most beautiful beaches I've ever seen, *from a window.* Can't we take a walk? Just this once?"

Her pleading eyes were hard to resist. "I guess a short walk wouldn't hurt," he said softly.

They walked outside through the gardens to a path leading down to the shore. There were about a hundred couples at the resort and although not all of them were outside, it seemed that Dane and Reagan couldn't go more than a few steps without encountering someone kissing or embracing or at least holding hands.

Before they got to the water, they removed their shoes and left them by a rock pile. They stood at the water's edge for a while, content to let the waves lap at their feet. Then they began to walk.

There was about thirty minutes of daylight left, and it promised to be a beautiful sunset.

Dane drew in a deep breath and opened all of his senses to his surroundings. The ocean was myriad shades of blue and teal. Where it met the horizon was a deep sapphire giving way to peach, pink, and purple. The rhythmic crash of the waves soothed him, and his skin came to life as the sea breeze washed over him. He could smell the salt and taste its tang. Under different circumstances, he would enjoy this tropical paradise, especially if he were here with the right person. He stole a glance at Reagan, and waited for some kind of physical reaction to kick in, for his heart to accelerate, or his face to break into a grin, or to be overtaken by an irresistible urge to sweep her into his arms.

But none of those things happened. And if they had, he wouldn't have acted on them.

Dane's burner phone vibrated in his pocket. Besides Landon, there was only one person who had this number. Dane looked at the screen, and his heart sped up. *I hope this doesn't mean trouble at home.*

REAGAN

"I NEED TO take this in private," Dane said. They had gone far enough that no one else was nearby. "Hold on," he said into the phone. Then he turned and walked away.

Dane had a burner phone for Landon to keep in touch with them, and he'd given one to Reagan too, just in case they got separated. She didn't know if Dane had given his burner number to anyone else. If it was Landon, she was sure Dane wouldn't leave her out of the conversation. Dane kept his back to her for several minutes, then began pacing back and forth, while still talking. His face was somber.

Reagan studied his profile and felt a little regretful for the times she'd snapped at him today. They'd been together in close proximity for five days now. That was something Reagan wasn't used to, and she supposed Dane wasn't, either.

He disconnected the call, and Reagan thought he would walk back her way, but instead he put his hands in his pockets and stared out over the ocean. The muted oranges, pinks, and purples had given way to a blaze of color, but Reagan sensed that he wasn't even seeing it. She sat down on the sand.

Ten minutes passed. It was almost dark, and he still hadn't moved. Reagan finally approached him. "Is everything okay? Was that Landon?"

She got the feeling that he'd forgotten about her. "No, it wasn't him." Dane said, and took off walking. Reagan trailed after him. By the time they got back to where they'd left their shoes, it was almost too dark to find them.

Dane didn't say a word the whole time, and once they got into the building where Reagan could see his face, it was expressionless. He swiped the key card in their door and held it open for her to go through.

He locked the door behind them and went to his suitcase in the closet where he hid the bug tracker. After he'd swept the room, he sat down on the edge of the bed. He folded his hands over his knees and didn't say anything for a moment.

"I need to tell you something," Dane said.

He didn't say anything, and Reagan steeled herself.

He took a breath. "I have a son."

That was the last thing Reagan expected him to say. For once, she was at a loss for words. "I—I had no idea, Dane." Her heart began to race. "That phone call—is he okay?"

For the first time since he'd gotten the phone call, Reagan felt like he saw her. His features softened. "Yes, he's fine. Thanks." Dane let out a breath. "I—I'm sorry I didn't tell you about this earlier."

"It's okay," Reagan said. "It's not like we're really married or even dating. Your personal life isn't my business." She sat beside him, leaving some space between them.

He ran a hand through his hair and sighed. "So. I—uh, yeah. His—well, his mother and I met about six years ago in Miami. She—we, had a very brief fling and then she found out she was pregnant." He hung his head and wiped his hand across his mouth. "And we got married. We haven't lived together since he was a couple of months old. We—it just didn't work. But I help support him, and we, well, we sort of co-parent him."

"I'm sorry, Dane. I didn't know you were divorced."

He twisted the wedding band around on his finger. "Well, we never did get divorced. She—she wanted the protection of marriage, and even though I was pretty certain we'd never reconcile, I wanted my son's parents to be married." He winced and shook his head. "I'm sure that doesn't make any sense."

Protection of marriage? That's an odd phrase, Reagan thought. "It doesn't have to make sense to me," she said. They sat in silence for a few moments.

"What's his name?" Reagan asked softly.

Dane smiled. "Danny. He's five." His features softened. "He's my whole world. I'm crazy about him."

Reagan smiled back. "That's wonderful, Dane. I'm glad you're in his life."

Dane stood and began to pace, and rammed his hands through his hair. "Well, I'm about to be a much bigger part of his life. His mother is dead. That's what that phone call was about."

Reagan felt her jaw drop, and her heart sped up. "Dane, that's awful. I'm so sorry." So technically, he was a widower now. It was hard for Reagan to wrap her head around that.

Dane rubbed a hand across one eye. "Reagan—she, she overdosed. My—Danny's mother was, um, Blayze."

Reagan frowned. "Blaze?"

"With a *y*. Blayze, you know—the—"

Reagan gasped. "*Blayze*? The supermodel?" Dane nodded. Her jaw dropped again. "You were married to *Blayze*?"

Dane looked at her somberly. "I know it's hard to believe. Her real name was Sally Ann. I've actually had Danny for more of his life than she has, and completely for most of the last year. She was starting to get into the party circuit again, and I refused to let her be anywhere around him when she was messing with that stuff." Reagan's mind was still reeling at his revelation.

He sat again next to her and put his head in his hands. "She tried, especially at first, but she was never cut out to be a mother. Her life growing up was such a mess, she didn't have any role models or anything normal to reference." He sighed. "I tried so hard to convince her to get help. Money wasn't an issue and she could have paid for the best rehab program anywhere in the world, ten times over. But in the end, she just didn't want it."

Reagan hesitated, then laid her hand on his back. "I'm so sorry, Dane. I'm sorry for Danny," she clarified. "No little boy should have to go through losing his mom, no matter what the circumstance." A feeling of great sadness washed over her. "Was he with her—?" She let the question trail off.

Dane straightened up a little and shook his head. Reagan's hand fell away. "No, fortunately, no. He's been with my brother since I left Florida with you. He and Landon are the only ones who have the number for my burner phone."

"Where does your brother live?"

"Miami. He's a—don't laugh. He's a pastor."

Reagan burst out laughing, then covered her mouth. "I'm sorry."

He smirked and shook his head. "I know. Anyway, he's a big part of Danny's life, too, so that's good. Very stable."

"Is Danny with your brother and his family now?"

"Shane doesn't have a family."

"Shane? Your brother's name is *Shane*?" Reagan fell back on the bed and broke into peals of laughter. "They named you Shane and Dane. I hope *your* parents never meet *my* parents!" She took a breath and sat up. Dane was just sitting there with a goofy grin on his face, shaking his head.

"Yeah, I thought about that when I met Landon and Brandon," he said. He rolled his eyes. "Our parents would probably become best friends." They sat in silence, each wrapped in their own thoughts.

Dane put his head in his hands and made a frustrated noise. "I can't believe—she—I, I'm really not feeling grief right now. Shouldn't I be overwhelmed with grief? But the woman I loved ceased to exist a long time ago. I think I'm— I think I'm angry. Yes, I'm angry. Does that make me a terrible person?" Reagan thought these were rhetorical questions, and he just needed to process his feelings.

Dane stood and began to pace back and forth. "Did she even think about—about what this would do to her *son*?" He looked devastated. "He won't even—he won't even remember her," he said, his voice nearly a whisper.

"I'm so sorry," Reagan murmured. She wished there was something she could do or say.

Dane blinked rapidly. "I need to—I'm going for a walk."

Reagan understood that he needed some time alone. "I'll see you in the morning, then."

Without another word, he left.

12

DANE

DANE HARDLY SLEPT that night. A long walk on the beach usually calmed him, but his emotions were still stirred up. He lay in bed for a long time thinking about Sally Ann and their brief, tempestuous marriage. At first, they'd both wanted to make it work. Dane was deeply in love with her—or at least the Sally Ann side that she showed to him. The Blayze side was disturbing and dark, and Dane wanted nothing to do with her. Unfortunately, that side fought a hard battle and ultimately won possession of Sally Ann's soul.

Dane had always held out hope that she would leave the toxic world of high fashion, turn back into Sally Ann, and make a family with him and Danny. As the years wore on, he finally accepted that it wasn't going to happen, but he never took steps to end the marriage, and neither did she. Now, he wasn't bound to her, even legally. *I'm a widower.* Dane always associated that word with older men. He couldn't wrap his head around the fact that he was now free to seek another relationship and even remarry someday.

In her business, Blayze liked being able to play the "husband card" when it suited her. If Dane was being honest with himself, he'd played the marriage card on occasion, too, if a woman showed interest. Honestly, he'd been burned and had a full enough life juggling his career with fatherhood. Danny was his priority, and he was going to be very careful about bringing a woman into his life.

He and Reagan were at breakfast, sitting by themselves in the corner. They'd purposely come late hoping to avoid the Carsons, and it almost worked. The perky couple was just leaving as Dane and Reagan sat down, and came over to say hello. They managed to keep the conversation short, and breathed a sigh of relief when the couple left.

"So, could I ask—where you met Blayze?" Reagan asked.

Dane lifted an eyebrow and took another forkful of his delicious omelet. "I never took you for a Blayze fan."

Reagan rolled her eyes. "I'm not—you know I'm not into all that fashion stuff. But—really, um, *Trey*, we're talking an *international* star here, not just any run-of-the-mill celebrity."

"Well, it's not really a very interesting story. I went to a club, she was there, and we left together." His face flushed.

"Did you recognize her?"

"No. She wore a disguise. She couldn't go out in public as herself."

Reagan nodded. Blayze had auburn hair and electric blue eyes. "That makes sense. So, what did she look like that night?"

Dane hemmed and hawed for a moment. "She—she was, she wore a wig with long, blond hair," he finally said. "And brown contacts."

"Ah," Reagan commented.

"What's that mean?"

"You have a type. You're attracted to brown-eyed blondes."

"If you say so," he smirked. "Her real name was Sally Ann Fogg. She was from Kentucky."

"So, how exactly did you meet her?"

Dane squirmed in his seat. "The same way everyone meets at a club."

Reagan shrugged. "I don't go to clubs."

"Well, I don't, either," he said. He scooted his chair back. "I'm going back for seconds. You want anything?"

Reagan gaped at him. "Are you having a growth spurt?"

"Is that a crack about my age?" Dane playfully cuffed her on the shoulder as he went past.

When he returned to the table, he dug into his food. Reagan was done with hers, and sipped at her coffee. "I still can't believe you and your brother have rhyming names."

"Yeah, that's pretty crazy."

"So, what will you name your next son?" Reagan teased. Her face immediately fell. "I'm so sorry! That was insensitive of me."

Dane smiled. "You're fine, Sara." He took a drink of his coffee. "Nothing that rhymes with *Danny,* that's for sure!" They both laughed. Then he grew thoughtful. "I didn't choose a responsible mother for my son the first time around, but if I get another chance, I'll be much more careful." His eyes locked with hers.

Reagan looked at him warily. "I sure hope you're not asking me to volunteer for the job!"

Dane almost spit out his coffee. "No," he said with a chuckle. "Definitely not."

Reagan let out an exaggerated sigh of relief. "Good. Glad we're in agreement on that," she said with a grin.

Dane's phone vibrated in his pocket. "It's Shane," he whispered to Reagan. "Shane, what's up? Is everything okay?"

His brother's voice reassured him. "Danny's fine. Absolutely fine, I promise. But you told me to call if anything looked fishy."

"What's going on?" Dane exchanged a worried look with Reagan.

"Someone must have leaked that he's here with me. I have reporters calling, and some of them are starting to gather outside. It's not paparazzi-level, but it might get there."

Dane ran a hand through his hair. "You haven't said anything to a reporter, right?" He instantly regretted the words. "Shane—I'm sorry, I didn't mean that."

His brother's soothing voice came down the line. "No worries. I haven't said a word, and I've stopped answering the phone for now. We're fine here, we'll hunker down. I just wanted to let you know."

Dane felt panic rising in his chest. *What have I done? My son just lost his mother, and I—*"Shane, I need to see him."

"Aren't you out of the country?"

Dane's mind spun. "Yes. Hold on. Give me a moment." He closed his eyes and weighed all the implications of bringing Danny to St. Jardin. "I want you to bring him here.

It won't be a long plane ride, and it will be completely safe. I can't use a credit card right now, but if you buy the tickets and get him here, I'll pay you back—"

"Dane, I'll handle it. For starters, tell me what country you're in," he said drily.

"St. Jardin."

"Really? I've always wondered if it's as beautiful as people say. I'll let you know when I find a flight."

Dane thought about the taxi choices at the airport, and didn't want his son subjected to any of that. "Rent a car when you get here," he said. "I'll text you the address where I'm staying." No way was he going to explain that it was a honeymoon resort, or anything about Reagan. There'd be time for all of that later. Dane let out a deep breath. "Shane, thanks so much." He was fortunate to have a brother who would drop everything to do this for him.

"You know I'll do whatever it takes to keep Danny safe."

"Be sure you're not followed when you leave." Dane felt helpless. He couldn't call on any of his usual sources to help his brother get out of the country undetected.

"You're not the only one with good contacts. We'll be fine."

Dane had an idea what Shane meant by that, and felt mildly relieved. He disconnected and let out a breath.

"They're coming here?" Reagan asked.

Dane nodded. "I can't—he's my son. I have to keep him safe. The paparazzi are starting to sniff around. They've made the connection between Danny and his mother and traced him to Shane."

Reagan put her hand on his and squeezed. He was surprised how much comfort he found in that simple gesture.

"Of course he should be here with you. It's private, and it's safe." She laid down her napkin. "Are you done? We can take some coffee back to the room and dig into our case again."

Dane sighed inwardly. He and Reagan would probably end up arguing over "their case" and not get anywhere. Honestly, he felt like he'd make more headway on his own.

They decided to detour back through the main lodge to stop at the coffee station. Rose was there in the lobby and called over to them. She wore a long, flowing tie-dye muumuu in shades of pink, and her Converse. "Yoo hoo, Sara! Did you get signed up for the spa day?" She handed Reagan a pamphlet.

Dane resisted the urge to laugh out loud. *Reagan, at a spa day?*

"No, I didn't," she replied. She opened the pamphlet and perused it. Dane was shocked at the next words that came out of her mouth. "I've never done anything like this. It sounds fun." She looped her arm through Dane's. "But I'm not sure I could spend a whole day away from my husband."

Maybe this was a blessing in disguise. "You should go, honey. Really, it's okay." The endearment felt awkward rolling off his lips, and he hoped he didn't sound too eager to be rid of her.

Reagan looked surprised. "You're sure?"

"Yes, I'm sure. But of course I'll miss you," he added. Dane patted her arm and began to step away, and felt Rose's blue-eyed gaze on him.

"Whatever will you do with yourself all day, Trey?"

"Ah—well, I brought a great book to read. Maybe I'll go lay on the beach and—read it." Why did he feel like she could see right through him? He leaned down and planted a kiss on the top of Reagan's head. "Have fun. I'll see you later this afternoon. Love you," he added. *I hope I sound like a devoted husband.* He smiled and waved at the ladies and left.

Dane got back to the room, locked the door, and swept it for bugs. He got all of his equipment set up and settled in. Then he realized he'd forgotten his coffee. He yawned. *Oh well, I'll take a break later.*

He stared at the computer screen for a long time. *Maybe I've been going at this from the wrong angle.* He went through all his notes on Navarro again. Then he decided to get a hold of one of his confidential informants to see if he'd heard anything. It would be risky, but Dane was willing to take that chance.

Dane went to a completely dark web site, navigated through a bunch of back doors while covering his tracks, and finally got where he wanted to be. He pulled up Buzzy's handle and was relieved to see that he was online. Dane typed: *Need more on N's recent activities. 6.* It was heavily encrypted and Buzzy would need to use their sixth encryption series to unravel it.

Dane leaned back and stretched his arms above his head while he waited for a response. He thought about what his and Danny's future would look like without his mother. Sally Ann didn't have any family, so Dane wouldn't have to worry about that. He knew his parents and brother would continue to be the support network he needed to help raise Danny. Dane sighed. He really needed to start going back to church. Danny went with Shane sometimes and loved it.

His thoughts were interrupted by a reply from Buzzy. Dane went to work right away and was stunned when he decoded it. *Look into Phil Diamond,* it said. *That's all I can give you.*

Phil Diamond? Dane searched his memory. *Isn't that the guy who runs Diamond Pharmaceuticals?* They were based in Florida. Not one of the biggest pharma companies, but they held their own, and they had a good reputation. After a few clicks, Dane had some very up-to-date information. Since the trade embargo with Cuba had been relaxed, Diamond had been sending teams of scientists there to share research and equipment. Nothing wrong with that. How could Diamond be connected to Doug Navarro?

But then one sentence in an interview quoting Phil Diamond piqued Dane's interest. *"Cuba's state-run health care system has access to some promising anti-cancer drugs that aren't yet available in the US. We hope to collaborate with Cuban scientists to make those available to us for clinical trials and pave the way for FDA approval."* The article had been published by the *Miami Herald* about a month ago. The reporter who conducted the interview was Reagan St. Clair.

13

*WEDNESDAY
MIAMI, FLORIDA*

SARA

SARA FLEW OUT of Chicago early Wednesday morning.
Her dad drove her to the airport and she felt terribly guilty
for deceiving him, even if it was just a little white lie. *Going
to Miami instead of Orlando is just a teeny little lie, right?*

Her direct flight landed in Miami just before noon. She
had a long layover that would give her plenty of time to get
everything done. The first unknown factor in her plan was
whether Reagan had changed the code on her apartment
door. Sara had stayed there for two nights last year during
spring break, and for a week between Christmas and New
Year's just a few months back. She and Reagan got some
sister time while their parents stayed at a hotel. Fortunately,
the code was the same. She was relieved to not have to ask
the building manager to let her in.

The biggest hurdle to overcome was to find Reagan's
passport. Sara didn't even know if it was at the apartment,
but she was betting on the fact that since Reagan was in
disguise, she had left Florida without it. If it wasn't there,

83

Sara's last resort would be to call Landon, come clean, and demand that he get her passport back from Reagan and overnight it to Orlando. Because Sara was *not* going to miss this chance to sing with Disney.

Sara was uncomfortable at the prospect of rifling through her sister's things, but decided to ask for forgiveness later instead of permission now. To her great relief, it was in the second desk drawer she opened, in plain sight.

Sara adjusted the baseball cap on her head. She had bought a brunette wig and fashioned it into a long braid after securing her own hair under an elastic nylon cap. The baseball cap gave her an added layer of security. She walked through the apartment house lobby, pulling two large roller bags behind her, complete with her sister's luggage tags. Sara's ID was tucked away in one of her suitcases, she now had Reagan's passport in her purse, and was outfitted in some of her clothes, right down to her Birkenstocks. She tossed in an extra set of Reagan's jeans and a t-shirt just in case.

She avoided eye contact with the doorman, who smiled and held the door for her. "Did you call an Uber, Ms. St. Clair?" He asked, gesturing to a black SUV.

First test passed with flying colors! "Yes, thank you," Sara said quietly, averting her face. The less said, the better. He helped load her suitcases in, and she climbed into the backseat.

She would spend only one night in St. Jardin. As soon as her flight landed, Sara would go to the resort, switch passports with Reagan, and get a hotel for the night. She had an early morning flight and would be in Orlando by noon tomorrow to begin her adventure.

Best of all, her brothers would be none the wiser. Sara

would call Landon tomorrow, or maybe she'd just let Reagan take care of it. If Reagan was posing as a newlywed bride, Sara wondered who her groom was. Probably some guy from work. All her sister ever did was work. Sara didn't think she'd even gone on a date in over a year.

Sara was really proud of herself for planning this without any help. She'd been meticulous about the details. The only thing she hadn't been able to do is add a dozen years to her face, but she didn't think that was a problem. *Being an adult isn't so hard after all,* she thought happily. She spent the rest of the ride dreaming about singing with the Disney show. This could be her big break.

Sara checked her bags through and got in line at security. *Now for the next test,* Sara told herself. *The one that really counts.* Getting past Reagan's doorman was one thing, airport security was entirely another. She flashed her passport when asked, and was waved on. *Whew.*

Now Sara could finally relax. She had plenty of time. She had thought about wandering around Miami before coming to the airport, but decided to play it safe. There was no worse feeling than running to catch a flight, and there was no room for error now. She got a late lunch and bought a magazine at one of the airport shops.

Sara sat and thumbed through the magazine for a while. She decided to use the restroom before her flight. She hated the microscopic bathrooms on planes. She glanced at the time. It would need to be quick. They would be boarding her flight in a little while.

When she came out of the ladies' room, she turned right and then realized she was going the wrong way, so she quickly made a u-turn.

And slammed right into someone. A tall, masculine someone.

"Oh! I'm sorry," she sputtered as she retreated and regained her footing.

The tall, dark-haired man looked startled for a second, and then he looked deeply into her eyes. Everything around Sara went into slow motion and then telescoped down to the two of them, no one and nothing else.

And for several seconds, time stood still.

He reached out and gently touched her arm. "Are you okay?" he asked with a look of concern.

Sara's face burned. "I'm fine, thanks."

She left as quickly as she dared, found a quiet corner, and hunched down in her seat. Reagan was a somewhat recognizable figure in Miami, and the last thing Sara needed was to call attention to herself. Her mind wandered back to the man she'd bumped into. He sure was handsome, but much too old for Sara. *What am I thinking? I'm about to embark on a new adventure. I don't have time for romance.*

A couple of times, Sara felt like someone was watching her, but figured she had an overactive imagination. Finally, her flight was called. She walked across the tarmac and boarded the staircase of the small, twin engine aircraft. Landon and Kelsea had been to St. Jardin multiple times and said they always flew into the island's airport on regular jets, but Sara didn't have the luxury of time, and took the first flight she could get.

It looked like the plane had about thirty seats. Sara was in the last row on the left, across from the handsome man and a little red-haired boy. That must be his son. She didn't recall seeing him when she bumped into the man, but then again, she was focused only on his dark good looks, his kind, sparkling eyes, and his gentle touch on her arm. Sara's face burned with embarrassment. She averted her gaze and slid into the window seat and buckled in.

The flight attendant came through the cabin to make one final check before takeoff. "This seat is empty," she said, tapping the seat next to Sara. That was fine with her. She was tired and planned to sleep for the ninety-minute flight, so she was happy that she would have the armrest to herself.

Sara watched Miami disappear as the plane climbed higher in the sky. Within seconds, they were completely over the water. She continued staring out at the ocean until she felt a movement next to her. It was the little boy from across the aisle.

"Hi! I'm Danny," he said with a gap-toothed grin.

"Hi, I'm—" Sara paused. "I'm Sara." It wouldn't matter which name she shared with a little boy.

"Wanna see my Legos?" He pulled out a little carrying case especially made for them from of his backpack.

Sara looked past him and met those warm brown eyes and engaging smile. "Is it okay?" he called over. "If he's bothering you, please tell me."

There was no wedding ring on his left hand.

Sara took a breath. "He's fine," she said with an answering smile.

"Send him back when you're tired of him," the man said. Sara was happy to give Danny's dad a break.

Sara smiled and helped Danny fasten his seat belt. Over the next half hour, he was so engaging that Sara forgot she was tired. He told her all about his Legos and then moved on to talk about his other favorite toys, his friends at daycare, his neighbor's dog, Dexter, and how excited he was to start kindergarten soon. He was just adorable and seemed to have the attention span of a gnat. He reminded Sara a little of her niece, Shelbie.

They played a little card game and then he pulled out a coloring book and some markers, and invited Sara to color a picture with him. When they finished, Danny put everything away and pulled out an iPad, slapped the headphones on, and started to watch a cartoon. The flight attendant brought sparkling water for Sara and apple juice for Danny.

As soon as the plane began its descent, Danny's dad motioned to him to come back over, and Sara helped him pack up his things. "I enjoyed meeting you, Danny."

"Bye, Miss Sara. Thank you for playing with me."

For a moment, Sara wondered if Danny's dad used him as a way to meet women, and half expected Danny to ask for her e-mail or phone number. But he simply darted back to his seat and let his dad fasten his seat belt.

"Thanks, Miss Sara," the man echoed. He really did have the most beautiful smile, but it appeared this was a chance encounter, nothing more.

Sara stared out the window as they got closer and closer to the ground—at least she hoped the pilots could see some land, because they were still over complete darkness, which she assumed was water. Before she knew it, they were racing down the runway, and slowed to a stop.

Now, her real work would begin. Sara rehearsed her speech to Reagan and hoped her sister wouldn't be angry with her for following her to St. Jardin. Maybe she would let Sara sleep in her room at the resort so Sara wouldn't have to spend money on a hotel room.

You've got this. You're an adult. And by this time tomorrow, you'll turn the page on a brand new chapter.

14

WEDNESDAY NIGHT
ST. JARDIN AIRPORT

SHANE

SHANE COLLECTED HIS and Danny's luggage off the carousel and got in line at the rental car counter. St. Jardin's airport was small, and it was only a few steps from one area to the other. "Stay right with me, buddy," he said to Danny, who was singing to himself and looking around.

Shane saw "Miss Sara" still standing near the carousel, and couldn't stop thinking about her. When the beautiful little brunette collided with him in the airport, he was fairly certain he recognized the *Herald* reporter, Reagan St. Clair. Shane had never met her in person, but he had a general sense of what she looked like and had seen her a couple of times from afar at crowded events. When you saw that dark braid, plaid shirt, and Birkenstocks, there was no mistaking who it was.

So many thoughts had collided in Shane's mind during those few seconds. First, how lovely she was, how beautiful her sparkling brown eyes were, and that up close, she was much younger than he expected. Then, he immediately wondered if she had arranged their "chance" meeting to get close to Danny, but then he answered his own question in the next breath—a top-tier investigative reporter like Reagan St. Clair would never be chasing a story about Blayze, no matter how compelling, and she couldn't have gotten through to the secure area without a boarding pass, anyway. There were no photographers around her, and if he'd suspected in the very least that she was up to something, he'd have whisked his nephew out of there in a heartbeat. On the plane, she was sweet as could be, and Shane didn't have any qualms about Danny sitting with her.

In all his years ministering to the people on the streets of Miami, Shane had met people from all walks and stations of life, from the downtrodden and broken to some of South Florida's most successful and famous athletes, politicians, and business moguls who came to volunteer at his church and associated ministries—some of them for a photo op and some out of a sincere wish to give back. Shane had the spiritual gift of discernment, and had good instincts concerning people. Still, he couldn't figure Reagan out.

Why was she calling herself *Sara*? Something wasn't adding up, even how sweet she seemed to be. Reagan St. Clair had the reputation for being a real no-nonsense scrapper. Maybe she was on a big story and was playing a part. And maybe when he got back to Miami he'd look her up and find out what this business was all about. *Just to make contact as an interested member of the community,* he told himself.

He watched Reagan wrestle a large suitcase off the carousel, roll it back a few feet, and then pull it behind her. She must be waiting for more of her luggage. Shane's heart tripped. *Hey, we could offer her a lift.* Just then, a tall, muscular man in jeans and a black t-shirt stepped next to her, put his arm around her shoulder, and leaned in close to talk to her.

So, she'd come to St. Jardin to meet a man. Shane felt a surprising spear of disappointment. *She's too young for you, anyway.*

"May I help you, sir?" The young woman at the rental car counter was speaking to him. Shane handed over the required documents and glanced down at his nephew.

Where was Danny? Shane's heart began a crazy dance. He whirled around and saw Danny crouched down behind Reagan's large suitcase, as if he were hiding. "Danny!" he called. The little boy looked up and skipped back over to his uncle. Reagan and the man hadn't even known he was there.

Shane squatted down and hugged Danny as his heart returned to its regular rhythm. "You have to stay right by me," he said. "Don't do that again."

Danny hung his head. "I was gonna hide and then say *surprise* to Miss Sara. And say goodbye to her again."

Poor little fellow. He's had enough loss lately. It won't hurt to take a moment to tell her goodbye. Shane signed the rental agreement and took the car keys. "Okay, now we can—" he turned and looked at where Reagan had been standing, but she and the man were gone. A whole new wave of travelers flooded the baggage claim area. Well, that was that. "Come on, buddy, we're going to go see Daddy now."

"Oh goody! Yay, yay, yay!" Danny cheered, skipping ahead of Shane. It appeared that he was able to forget about "Miss Sara" very quickly.

It was too bad that Shane couldn't do the same.

15

SARA

SARA LET OUT a breath. She was home free. After arriving in St. Jardin, she filled out the paper immigration and custom form and cleared immigration. She didn't have anything to declare, and now she was waiting for her second suitcase to appear on the carousel when she heard a man's voice next to her. "Welcome to St. Jardin, Ms. St. Clair," he said softly.

Why did someone here know her name? Did he mean Reagan? Sara swallowed and glanced up at the man. His expression didn't look welcoming at all. Her heart began to pound. *How would he know that Reagan was coming here?* Sara was confused. No one at all should have known that either she *or* Reagan were coming here.

Suddenly, she felt the man's arm come around her, and something hard pressed into her side. Icy fear snaked through her veins. "Give me your phone," he whispered, and Sara handed it over. An announcement came over the PA, and he spoke a little louder into her ear. "You'll be coming with me. Mr. Rogers can't wait to see you."

Sara's heart began to beat wildly. *What was going on?* "Who is Mr. Rogers?" she asked sharply, and winced as the discomfort in her side turned to pain. Tears sprang to her eyes.

"Which suitcase is yours?" the man hissed into her ear.

"Th-th-the blue one," she stammered, gesturing to the carousel.

"We'll get it together," he said. He lowered his voice. "My associates are stationed at every door, so don't try anything." His tone convinced Sara that he meant business. Her gaze darted to two doors that she could see, and a nondescript, muscular man stood at each. *Dear heaven, what is going on with my sister?*

Sara wondered if Danny and his dad were still around. Maybe she could signal to them somehow. She looked around as dozens of people spilled into the baggage claim area. At least one other flight must have just arrived.

"Don't even think about it," the man said in a clipped voice, and Sara's fleeting hope evaporated. The man grabbed one suitcase and motioned to Sara to get the other. He latched on to her arm in a vise grip and propelled her out a door, where a black SUV was waiting. "Let's go."

Lord, help me.

16

DANE

DANE HURRIED REAGAN through dinner so they could go for a quick walk on the beach. He was anxious to grill her in private about her interview with Phil Diamond.

"The seaweed wrap was amazing," she gushed as they exited the main building and headed for the beach. "I'm definitely finding a place in Miami to do that again when I get home." Dane resisted the urge to roll his eyes. Reagan hadn't stopped talking about the spa day since she finished up, just a few moments before meeting him for dinner.

He took her hand to hurry her along and looked around to ensure that they were alone. "Reagan, I need to talk with you before Shane and Danny get here. I made some progress on the case." He quickly caught her up. "I asked one of my CIs for something more on Navarro, and he told me to look into Phil Diamond."

Reagan frowned. "From Diamond Pharmaceuticals? I just interviewed him."

Dane nodded. "I know. I read the article."

"Diamond's legit. Why would he and Navarro be connected?" Reagan removed an elastic hair tie from her wrist and caught her blond hair up in a ponytail as the wind whipped it around her.

"I don't know, but it's definitely interesting. Here's one scenario: what if Navarro is trying to get his hands on some of the anti-cancer drugs from Cuba to conduct illegal trials in the US? That would totally be his MO and explain why he's working with a group of businessmen. Conduct the trials, find out which drug or drugs has the best results, and then buy it cheap before it goes on the market, and make a killing. Or better yet, send a group of mercenaries into Cuba to take over the lab where it's manufactured."

Reagan stopped walking. "But how is the governor connected?'

Dane's head was beginning to pound. He still refused to believe that a man he'd known and admired his whole life could be involved with this. He felt his phone vibrate, and picked up.

"We're just leaving the airport," Shane said. "What room are you in?" Dane gave him the address to his "hotel," but couldn't bring himself to reveal that it was a honeymoon resort.

"Two-twelve," Dane said. "Shane—I need to explain, I'm here undercover—"

"No time," his brother interrupted. "My phone's almost dead. See you soon." He disconnected.

Dane let out a huge sigh. No telling what Shane's reaction would be. He turned back toward the resort and pulled Reagan with him. "They're on their way in from the airport. I need to make sure I put everything away." He'd come back to the lobby to meet Shane and Danny. That way he could explain Reagan to Shane before they met.

When they got back to the room, Reagan disappeared into the bathroom and a few minutes later, he heard the shower running. *What was she doing?*

Dane finished putting his notes away, then walked over to the closed door. "Reagan, why are you in the shower? They'll be here soon. I'm going down to the lobby to wait for them."

"Hold on! I'll be right there. I want to go with you. I have to let the conditioner set for another two minutes."

Dane buried his head in his hands and groaned. Since when had Reagan become so—so *fussy* about all these girl things? He bet that she'd never used conditioner once in her life before this week. He walked out onto the balcony and stared out over the ocean. Then he came back in, walked to the fridge, took out a bottle of water, and gulped half of it down. "Reagan, I'm going downstairs," he said.

A knock came at the door, and Dane groaned again. *That can't be them. Either they were halfway here when Shane called, or they made good time.* He set his water bottle down. As soon as he put his hand on the knob, the bathroom door opened, and out walked Reagan in a short terry-cloth robe, her head wrapped in a towel.

"Oh good, maybe they're here."

And you're half dressed. Dane thought. This wasn't going to go well. Because Shane was a pastor, he took pains to avoid any situation that could be misinterpreted. And if there was *any* situation that fit the bill, this was it. Dane turned the knob and sent a quick, desperate prayer heavenward. He hadn't really talked to God in a while, but the urge to do so came instinctively.

As soon as he opened the door, Danny let out a squeal and Dane squatted down. "Daddy!" Danny launched himself into Dane's arms

Dane closed his eyes and wrapped his arms around his little son, breathing in his unique little-boy essence. He rose to his feet, bringing Danny up with him. "Uh, hi," he said to his brother, who was staring at Reagan, who was staring at Dane.

Dane could see the wheels spinning in his brother's head as he took in the room, the bed, Reagan, and the wedding band on Dane's left hand that rested on Danny's head.

"You're married? *Since yesterday?*" Shane asked, his expression incredulous.

"Ah—no. Shane, this is Reagan St. Clair." He figured his brother, being from Miami, would at least know who she was, and might be impressed to meet a local quasi-celebrity.

"Reagan St. Clair?!" Shane exclaimed. He put his hands on his hips. "Dane, whoever this is, she's an impostor!"

"An imposter?" Dane and Reagan exclaimed in unison.

Reagan glared at Shane. "You have no idea what you're talking about!"

"Well, I'm from Miami, and I know what Reagan St. Clair looks like. And she was on my flight—our flight," he said, with a nod toward Danny. "But she was calling herself Sara. Trying to be incognito, I guess."

"I liked Miss Sara," Danny said. "She played games with me and we colored a picture."

Dane set his son down and quickly moved to Reagan, who looked like she might faint. Her face had gone white.

"Dane," she said, reaching for him. He grasped her around the waist and guided her to the loveseat.

"We'll figure it out," he said softly. Dane put his hand on Reagan's shoulder and looked at his brother. "This really is Reagan St. Clair. She's been working a case with me, and we had to go underground, which is why we're here."

Shane glowered at Reagan. "Do you know how old he is?" he shoved his thumb at Dane.

"You've got to be kidding!" Reagan shouted. "We're *not* married!"

"Great, so he's just your boy toy?" Shane said with a look of disgust.

Reagan glared at him. "You are *so* out of line! This is none of your business—"

A whistle cut the air. Dane cocked his head at Danny, who was looking out the sliding-glass door through his cupped hands, oblivious to the adults' conversation. "We'll talk about this later." He tried to put his thoughts in order. "Shane, tell me about the woman on the plane. It's important," he implored.

Shane ran a hand through his dark hair. "She looked like Reagan St. Clair, she had a long, dark brown braid, and wore a baseball cap, jeans, a plaid shirt, and sandals." He looked at Reagan. "I've seen you a couple of times on local TV and once at a Dolphins game, but I've never met you." His eyes narrowed. "Now that I look at you, I'm sure she was quite a bit younger."

"Yeah, I get that part. I left my AARP card at home," Reagan snapped. She looked at Dane. "Sara must have been wearing a wig." She removed the towel from her head. Her damp blond hair tumbled past her shoulders.

"Reagan is in disguise," Dane explained. "She dyed her hair blond and we brought her here under her sister, Sara's, passport, without her knowledge."

Shane frowned. "Is that even legal?"

Dane continued. "Reagan's—our attorney arranged it. Sara is a blonde—and yes, she's quite a bit younger than Reagan."

"Does Sara live in Miami?" Shane asked.

"No, she's from up north," Dane said.

Shane looked at Reagan. "Why would she disguise herself as you and come to St. Jardin?"

Reagan put her head in her hands and then looked up at Dane. "She must have found out that I had her passport," she said. "Brandon probably blabbed." Then her eyes widened. "She knows my door code. I bet she went to my apartment, got my passport, disguised herself, and flew here as me. But *why?* We need to get a hold of Landon."

"Wait," Dane said. He looked at Shane. "Did you see Sara leave the airport? Did she say where she was going? Did you see her get a taxi, or rent a car?"

Shane's eyes grew wide. "She—oh, wow. No, she didn't tell us why she was coming here. I didn't really talk with her. The seat next to hers was empty, and Danny sat there for most of the flight." He looked at Reagan apologetically. "I was going to offer her a ride, but she left the St. Jardin airport with a man. Who's Brandon? Who's Landon?"

"A man?" Reagan exclaimed. She jumped to her feet. "She doesn't know anybody here! Dane, what are we going to do?"

Dane felt a tug on his pant leg. "Daddy, I'm hungry."

Dane squatted down so he was eye-to-eye with his son.

"Oh, buddy, I'm sorry," he said. He looked at Reagan. "We don't have anything to eat here, do we?" She shook her head.

Reagan started pulling clothes out of a drawer. "I'm going to look for her."

Dane quickly stood and went to her. "You'll be playing into their hands," he said. He held her arms. "Reagan, you have to stay here. Let me handle this." They stared at one another for a few charged seconds, and then she deflated like a balloon.

"All right."

Dane grabbed his burner phone and took Danny by the hand. He spoke rapidly to the two adults. "I'm almost out of international minutes on this. I underestimated how many I'd need. I'm going to the front desk to use their phone to call Landon collect. I'll find Rose and Ike and ask them to get Danny some food." He hoped his unspoken message conveyed that he would trust no one else with his son. He turned to Shane. "I need you to text me a description of the guy that Sara left with, and any other details that you can remember from the moment you met her—anything she said, anything she did."

Dane thought of something else. "You're sure you and Danny weren't followed?"

Shane looked at him evenly. "I told you, I have resources, too."

Of course he did. But Dane didn't need to know the particulars. Finding Sara St. Clair was his priority now. He took a breath. "Reagan, promise me you'll stay here, for now. Don't even leave the room until I can figure some things out. He moved close to her. "*And get dressed,*" he hissed.

Reagan crossed her arms in front of her. "Is *he* going with you?" She glared at Shane.

"No, he's going to stay here to make sure you do." He looked at Shane, who looked as unhappy about the situation as Reagan did. "Try not to kill each other before I get back."

17

REAGAN

AS SOON AS the door closed behind Dane and Danny, Reagan made sure it was locked. Then she grabbed her clothes and marched into the bathroom without a word to the man standing in the middle of the room.

The nerve of him! Looking down his nose at her and jumping to all kinds of conclusions about her and Dane. Reagan's blood boiled as she tugged the brush through her damp hair. She laughed mirthlessly to her reflection in the mirror. He was a pastor! *That figures.* Reagan had met more holier-than-thou types than she could count, and had no use for them.

Reagan quickly dressed and spent the next ten minutes applying her makeup. She was starting to like how it made her feel, although she wished she knew how to do things with it so that she would look prettier and younger. Not that she cared one whit about Shane Corsica's insulting comment about her age.

When Reagan came back to the room, he was standing by the sliding glass door that he must have opened, staring out at the darkness. The pleasant tropical breeze drifted into the room.

"Just for the record, I don't have any designs on your brother," she said crisply. "I've known him for four years. We work together sometimes and he's a friend, end of story."

Shane shoved his hands in his pockets. "I overreacted, and I'm sorry," he said. "My little brother is all grown up, but you can tell I'm pretty protective of him." His brown eyes, so much like Dane's, held genuine contrition.

Reagan sat down in one of the chairs. "You asked who Landon and Brandon are. They're my brothers."

Shane's eyes grew wide, and he threw back his head and laughed. "Oh, no! That's unbelievable. I've never met any other brothers with rhyming names. I thought my parents were the only ones with a sense of humor."

He sure is handsome when he smiles. Reagan couldn't help smiling herself.

Shane sat in the other chair. "So, there are four of you?"

"Yes, I'm the oldest, then Landon and Brandon. The three of us were born within four years. And then Sara was my parents' surprise, when we were in our teens. Do you and Dane have other siblings?" She couldn't recall him ever speaking of anyone other than an older brother.

"No, I'm eleven years older than Dane. My mom had three miscarriages between us."

"That's too bad," Reagan replied. Suddenly, she felt uncomfortable, and jumped up. "Would you like some water?" she said as she walked over to the fridge.

"Sure, thanks." She handled him a bottle and uncapped

hers and drank deeply. "I wish Dane would get back. I can't imagine who my sister is out there with." She began to pace. "It should be me. They probably thought it *was* me."

"Well, you know Dane's one of the best minds out there. He'll figure this out," Shane said with confidence.

Reagan stopped mid-pace. "I have to look for her. I can't just sit here. Dane's *not* going to keep me on the sidelines," spat angrily. She turned abruptly, went to the desk, and began to gather the things she'd need. Suddenly, she felt a gentle touch on her arm.

"Hey," Shane said softly. Reagan stiffened, ready to do battle with him like she always did with Dane. But when she looked up, she didn't see challenge in his eyes. She only saw compassion.

"I can't imagine what I'd feel like if my brother was out there, helpless." He gave her a small smile and one eyebrow lifted. "Except that Dane wouldn't be helpless, because, you know, he's Dane." Shane looked at her apologetically. "I'm not doing a very good job at this." He seemed to study her more deeply. "You strike me as someone who thinks logically and has a great capacity to solve problems with just the right combination of thinking strategically and trusting your instincts."

Because of hers and Dane's disagreement earlier in the day, Reagan said the first thing that came to mind. "You don't think trusting your instincts is a bad thing?"

Shane shook his head. "No. In many cases, I think it's God-given. I think it can lead you to right conclusions. But if your emotions are deeply involved, they can compromise logical thinking and hijack the ability to interpret your gut instincts clearly."

Reagan couldn't believe how plainly he made his point without coming across as judgmental. "And I'm too emotionally involved in this," she murmured.

He nodded and gave her a gentle smile.

The frustration in her body dissipated, but was replaced by raw fear. "I just—if anything happens to her—" Reagan didn't cry often, and couldn't help the tears that came spilling out. "It's my fault. It's all my fault." She felt Shane's arms come around her. There was nothing inappropriate about his embrace. It was just one human being offering another solace, and Reagan felt immensely comforted.

"Shh," he whispered, and rubbed circles on her back. Then he began to pray in a conversational, soothing way. He prayed for God's protection over Sara and for Dane to have wisdom about what steps to take to find her. He prayed for Reagan to trust Dane's professional training and for her heart to be comforted so that she could be empowered to help bring about her sister's rescue.

When he whispered *Amen*, Reagan actually felt the burden lift from her shoulders. She'd never experienced anything like it. Shane took a step back and Reagan looked into his deep brown eyes. For a long moment, neither of them spoke. Finally, Reagan swallowed. "Thank you, Shane," she said.

"You're welcome."

Reagan excused herself to get a tissue. When she came back into the room, Shane had sat again.

Reagan was fascinated by him. "So, you're a pastor?"

He turned and looked at her. "Yeah. Yeah, I am."

"What church do you work for?"

Shane didn't say anything for several seconds. He leaned forward, elbows on his knees. "I run the Miracle Center."

The Miracle Center? Reagan plopped down into the chair. She couldn't believe it. The Miracle Center wasn't just a church. It was a gigantic organization that provided all kinds of services to the needy in Miami: transition housing for the homeless and recent parolees from prison, plus a prison ministry. A meal program that fed thousands. A rehab center. Job training and placement. A huge clothing and food distribution warehouse along with a department store that rivaled Walmart and Target. Free medical and dental services. After-school and tutoring programs for children and teens. A fleet of coffee shops. A sports program for teens. The list went on and on. Reagan had heard recently that they were making plans to open a small hospital. The Miracle Center had made a real difference in thousands of lives. It was legendary in Miami, and other cities had tried to replicate it, but only with marginal success. Miami's flagship organization outshone them all. It wasn't a church, but a ministry, and it had a mega-church with thousands of members at its center.

Reagan knew that one man had started the Miracle Center more than a dozen years ago and was at the helm of it all, but didn't know anything about him. And it would seem that he was sitting right here a few feet away from her.

"Wow—you're—" she couldn't even speak.

Shane grinned again. *That smile.* "Yep, that's me." He finished his water and tossed the empty bottle toward the trash can. It landed perfectly in the center.

"Do you really—do you really sleep only two or three hours a night, every night?" Reagan remembered reading that once.

Shane laughed. "Yes, that's true."

Reagan's face burned. *Of all the things to think of to ask him!* "I'm sorry, that was a silly thing to say." She giggled. *What is wrong with me? I* never *giggle.*

"If you'd like a tour sometime, I'd be happy to do that," he said.

I really shouldn't. "I'd like that," she heard herself say.

18

DANE

DANE PUT HIS key card in the door and braced himself. He had no idea what he would find in the room. Shane, tied to a chair perhaps, with a washcloth stuffed in his mouth? But they were just sitting there, talking. Knowing Shane, he had probably kept Reagan busy to take her mind off Sara.

Reagan shot out of her chair. "What did you find out?" Dane noticed that her eyes were a little red.

"Not much. Sara got a phone call yesterday from Disney, an invitation to tour with them this summer. She told the family that they were flying her to Orlando today to begin rehearsals. She left this morning."

"That's right," Reagan said. "She was going to do that last year but went to help Brandon with our nieces instead."

"She didn't say anything about going to Miami first. Landon didn't know anything about it." Dane reached for his laptop and opened it. "I'm going to see if I can trace her flight plan." He tapped on some keys and then grunted. "Yeah, she flew to Miami under her own name, and then she flew here using your passport, Reagan." He tapped some more keys and frowned. "She's booked from St. Jardin to Orlando tomorrow morning under her own name, so she must have been planning to come here to get her passport back. She must need it for the Disney gig."

Shane frowned. "You mean anyone can look up someone else's travel plans in a few seconds?"

Dane cocked an eyebrow at his brother. "I can."

"Oh," Shane responded. He drew the lone syllable out. "Where's Danny, by the way?"

"With the resort owners. I told them I would explain everything later. They were happy to spoil him and get him some food."

Shane stood and smiled. "Do you think they could spoil me and get me some food? Or does this place have a restaurant? I didn't get dinner, either."

"Oh, Shane, I'm sorry. Yes, I'm sure they could." Dane asked him to bring Danny back when they were both finished eating.

He locked the door behind his brother and turned to face Reagan. "I'm going out. I've got to get the airport security tapes so I can see who Sara left with. I know you want to be out there looking for your sister, but—"

"I'm fine staying here, for now. I know you'll put me to work when you're ready."

Who is this woman, and what has she done with Reagan? Dane sputtered, trying to think of something to say. He couldn't read Reagan's expression. It was some kind of cross between confidence and contentment.

"Go on. Get moving, Corsica," she said, giving him a push. He didn't have time to figure this out now. He grabbed jeans and a different shirt and headed for the bathroom to change. "Hey, wait a minute," Reagan said as he passed by her. "How are you going to get the tapes? You don't have any official jurisdiction here."

Dane grinned. "Remember? Someone told us to call on her if we needed *anything* while we're in St. Jardin. I'm going to see Louie at the Bahama Llama Boogie Shack, and find Moni."

19

SARA

I'VE NEVER BEEN so scared in my life. Two men were in the front, and the big man who escorted Sara got into the back seat with her. As soon as the doors of the black SUV closed, it roared away from the curb. Her stomach roiled. "Buckle up," he ordered. Sara put on her seat belt with shaking hands.

The man leaned over into her personal space, and her heart began to pound. He slipped a blindfold over her eyes and secured it. Sara held her breath. To her relief, the baseball cap held her wig securely in place.

"If you behave yourself, I won't need to use these," the man growled. Sara heard a clinking sound that might have been handcuffs.

As they drove, Sara tried to put her thoughts in order. *I'm on my own in a foreign country. No one knows I'm here. Do they even have an embassy here?* She swallowed back tears.

She would do anything right now to just be *Peanut* and have her family hovering over her.

Think, Sara. You're the only one who can help yourself out of this mess. She tried to remember specific things about the man who had approached her in the airport. He was tall and big, muscular, with dark hair, and dark skin or a tan. Was he Jardinian? Sara had no idea what a St. Jardin islander would look like. She wasn't even sure how he was dressed. It had all happened so fast.

Sara felt so disoriented with the blindfold. She tried to listen for external noises that could give her a clue to where they might be going, but the vehicle was well-insulated and all she could hear was muffled sounds.

It felt like they were on a twisting road. Their speed varied greatly and Sara had no idea how far they'd gone. Finally, they made a left turn and about fifteen seconds after that, a right, but that didn't mean anything to Sara, either. She was disoriented and didn't know if they'd traveled for a half hour or ten minutes.

The car made another left turn and slowed to a stop. After about ten seconds, Sara thought she heard some kind of electronic gate opening, and the vehicle began to move again, but very slowly. They traveled for at least another minute, by Sara's estimation. Were they on a small road, or a driveway?

The car came to a stop, and she felt the man lean into her space. His breath was warm on her cheek, and she held her breath. "We're here. Just so you know, we're completely isolated. If you try to scream or make a ruckus, there's no one around to hear you." Sara shivered as she felt him come closer. "And if you misbehave, I have a gag and handcuffs that I can use. You understand?" Sara nodded. She heard his door open and close. A few seconds later, her door opened and the man grabbed her arm and pulled her from the vehicle.

"Come on, walk with me," he ordered. It felt like they were on concrete. The first thing Sara heard was the ocean. The breeze was saturated and she could smell the salt in the air. Beyond that, she couldn't distinguish anything.

She thought they walked around the front of the vehicle. Then, she heard a door open. "Step up," the man said from in front of her. She followed him through the door and then he turned right. They might be in a hallway now. She strained to hear any sounds, but it was perfectly silent. After several seconds, the floor changed to carpet. They made two left turns, a right, another left, and then the man stopped.

"We're going into an elevator," he said quietly. The doors closed behind them with a soft *whoosh* and she could feel them ascending. Sara could tell that they were in a well-appointed car as opposed to a freight elevator. For some reason, that gave her comfort.

The doors opened quickly, and that told Sara that they weren't in a high-rise building. Would there even be skyscrapers on the island? It was still deathly quiet, and smelled like new paint. She followed the man down a thickly carpeted hallway, and then he stopped and she heard a door unlock. He guided Sara into the room and she heard the door close and lock. The man told her to sit. It felt like she was in a soft, luxurious upholstered chair. She heard the man moving around the room, and then he returned to her and removed the blindfold.

Sara blinked as her eyes adjusted to the soft light. She was shocked to realize that they were in what looked to be an opulent hotel room. The sight of the lavishly decorated king-sized bed filled her with panic, and her heart began hammering. The man pulled up a smaller chair and sat close to her, their knees almost touching. She memorized as much about him as she could: his battered tennis shoes, jeans, his plain black t-shirt. His black hair, glittering dark eyes and beard, the earrings in both ears. She could tell he had a lot of tattoos, but couldn't discern any detail.

"You'll stay here until Mr. Rogers arrives later tonight, Ms. St. Clair," he said. His English was heavily accented, but understandable. "He wants you to be comfortable, but you won't be permitted to contact anyone." He stared her down. "If you decide to cause any trouble, you'll face the consequences." He tipped his head at handcuffs, blindfold, and a gag that were laying on the table next to them.

Sara almost opened her mouth to ask who *Mr. Rogers* was again, and then it occurred to her that if they thought she was Reagan, that maybe Reagan was supposed to know him. No doubt it would be to her advantage for them to keep thinking that she was her sister. If Reagan were here, she wouldn't be scared out of her wits. *What would Reagan do and say?*

"I look forward to meeting with him," Sara said evenly. She kept her gaze steady on the man. Her mouth was so dry. "Could I get some water, please?"

The man got up, went over to a kitchenette, and opened a small fridge. When he came back, he held the bottle out, and then Sara saw a pistol in his other hand. "Just in case you thought of throwing the water in my face or something," he said. He tipped his head toward the door. "There are two more men outside the door, and they're armed, too," he said.

Sara sighed inwardly and uncapped the bottle. It appeared she was going to have to see this through.

"May I have my suitcases?" she asked. She already knew what the answer would probably be.

The man didn't blink, didn't move a muscle. "No."

Sara desperately hoped that the man or his associates wouldn't go through her luggage, although she held out little hope. Her driver's license and credit card bearing her real identity were tucked away in a pocket, and she knew they'd be found.

And if these people discovered who she really was, what would happen?

20

WEDNESDAY NIGHT

DANE

DANE CALLED FOR a taxi from his burner phone and told them to pick him up at the entrance to the resort, out on the main road. He didn't want the Goldmans or anyone else to see him leaving.

Fortunately, the taxi looked reliable and the driver looked older than sixteen. "Bahama Llama Boogie Shack," he said as he climbed in.

The man grinned. "You play poker with Louie?"

"Ah, no," Dane replied.

When the taxi pulled up to the restaurant, Dane looked at the building and thought there must be some mistake. But the neon sign and the life-sized llama statue bedecked in tropical flowers assured him he was at the right place. He went through the door and looked around the colorful two-story structure. He pegged Louie right away. He was the biggest, most exuberant guy there, clearly in charge.

"Welcome, amigo!" he exclaimed as he walked behind the bar. "What can I get for you?"

"Nothing right now, thanks," Dane said. "Are you Louie?"

The man grinned. "I sure am. And I know I can find something for you to drink that you will like!"

Dane smiled back. "Well, maybe later. I'm in a bit of a hurry right now. I'm actually looking for your niece, Moni. She told me—"

"Ah! You are her American friend! She told me all about you! Moni!" he shouted toward the back. The saloon doors opened and Moni swept out.

Her already happy face lit up. "Oh, sir, hello! So good to see you again!" She grabbed both of Dane's hands with hers. "You did meet Uncle Louie?"

"Yes, I did." Dane smiled at Louie. He touched Moni on the arm and lowered his voice. "You said to find you if I needed anything while I was here. Can we talk in private?"

"Of course, sir!" she replied in a stage whisper. She wiped her hands on a towel and set it down. "Come outside in back."

Dane followed her through the bar, down a hallway, and out the back door. As soon as the door closed, they found themselves in the quiet, tropical night air. "What can I do for you, sir?"

Dane smiled. "First of all, Moni, just call me Trey." Better to use his alias.

"Okay, sir Trey!"

That was even worse. "I need your help." Moni nodded enthusiastically. "I need to find someone, an American. It's very important. She left the airport a little while ago with a man, out one of the doors from the baggage claim area." Dane swallowed and lowered his voice. "I need to see the security tapes at the airport. Do you understand what I'm asking, Moni?"

"You want to steal the tapes?"

Dane closed his eyes. "No, no, not steal them. I just need to borrow them. Could you or Uncle Louie take me to see someone at the airport? Do either of you know anyone who works there who I could talk to?"

"Yes! I will make phone call! You wait here!" Before Dane knew what had hit him, she had slipped back inside the bar.

Oh Lord, what am I doing? Dane looked up and dragged his hands over his face. Then he began to pace.

A few minutes later, he heard a chugging noise coming from his left, and here came Moni and Sadie-belle. "Let's go, sir Trey!" Moni exclaimed. Dane got in and they took off in a cloud of exhaust. "I will take you to airport! We're going to see my brother, Gustav!" Dane decided not to ask how someone in Moni's Jardinian family ended up with the name *Gustav.*

It was a quick trip to the airport, and Moni chattered happily all the way. Dane's mind was on a hundred other details, and he had a hard time keeping up with her. As soon as they pulled up to the curb at the arrivals area, a tall youth with shoulder-length dark blond hair and gray eyes slid into the back seat, and Moni took off.

"This is Gustav!" she said. Dane and Gustav nodded to one another. Dane thought he might be a little older than Moni, but he sure didn't see any family resemblance.

"You have a phone?" Gustav asked Dane, and Dane

nodded. Gustav passed a device a little bigger than a phone to Dane. "Here is tapes from baggage claim for last two hours. If you find what you are looking for, you can transfer it to your phone. Then I have to take this back."

"We will ride around while you look!" Moni said.

"That's great, thanks," Dane said, and began surveying the tapes. With the information Shane had given him, it was easy to pinpoint the time frame. His heart went into overdrive as he saw Reagan—make that *Sara*—on the screen. Her disguise was unbelievably accurate. He saw her get her first suitcase off the carousel, and the man quickly joined her. Then Dane saw his little son come and crouch behind the suitcase for about twenty seconds, then he rejoined his Uncle Shane at the rental car counter. Soon, they left and more people began pouring into the area. The man and Sara got her other suitcase, and then, Dane lost them in the crowd.

After about fifteen seconds, he spied them again, and the man was holding tightly to Sara's arm and guiding her along. It looked like she was searching for someone—probably Shane and Danny. Unfortunately, the man seemed to know where all the security cameras were, and kept his face averted. Dane didn't find one good, clear shot of him.

As soon as he and Sara got outside, a black SUV slid up to the curb. In a matter of seconds, they loaded the luggage and Sara in, and were off. Dane looked at the SUV from every angle and was stunned to see that there were no license plates of any kind on it. "What the—" he murmured to himself.

"You find what you looking for?" Gustav said from over his shoulder.

"Yes, and no," Dane said, frustration starting to build. "This vehicle has no license plates." He saw Moni and Gustav exchange a look. "Does that mean anything to you?" Dane tried in vain to locate any other identifying marks on the vehicle. Even the make and model were missing.

"Ah—there is an underground syndicate that operates on the island," Gustav said. "All I know is they have power and the police are in their pocket. It is probably them."

Dane finished uploading the footage to his phone as they approached the airport again, and returned the device to Gustav. Moni stopped at the curb outside the departure area, and Gustav quickly unfolded himself from the back seat. "Thanks, Gustav," Dane said as he leaned out the window to shake his hand.

"You're welcome. Anything for my sister's friend." The young man smiled and waved as he went back into the airport.

Dane shook his head. "That was amazing, Moni," he said. "I'm very fortunate that your brother works in airport security. That was very helpful."

"Oh, Gustav no work in security," she said brightly. "He airport janitor."

21

WEDNESDAY NIGHT

REAGAN

REAGAN OPENED THE door to Shane and Danny. "Did you get something to eat?"

"Yes, they took good care of us," Shane replied. "The food was excellent."

"I had grilled cheese!" Danny said happily. "That's my favorite." He sat down on the bed and began bouncing up and down, singing the theme song from a kids' TV show about being a nice neighbor. He was a cute little guy and Reagan wondered if she could get to the point of feeling comfortable around him.

Reagan smiled at Shane. "The food here is outstanding," she said. "I didn't bring my running shoes, and I'm afraid I'll be a whale by the time we get home."

Shane raised an eyebrow. "I don't think you have anything to be worried about," he murmured.

Reagan felt herself blush. She couldn't think of anything to say and thankfully, at that moment, the door opened. It was Dane. He quickly locked it behind him.

"Hey, buddy!" he said, going to Danny and scooping him up. "How was dinner?"

"Good," Danny said, locking his arms around Dane's neck. "I got ice cream for dessert."

"Any luck?" Reagan asked.

"Yes and no," Dane said. He set Danny down on the bed. "Moni's down in the lobby, by the way. Her brother, Gustav, got me the airport surveillance tapes."

Reagan looked at him in confusion. "*Gustav?*"

Dane smiled and shook his head. "Long story for later," he said. "Anyway, we saw—uh, the person we were looking for leave with someone in an unmarked black SUV. No plates or other markings." Reagan glanced at Shane and knew he understood that Dane didn't want to bring up Sara in front of Danny. "I need to get online and check out some things and then see where we go from there." He walked over to the closet and got his equipment out. "Until I have more answers, we don't have anything to go on."

Reagan felt her eyes tearing up. "My sister is out there with—God knows who, and we don't have any way to find her?" Her stomach was tied in knots.

"I'm working on it, Reagan," Dane said.

"Daddy, can I go see Mr. Rogers?" Danny piped up.

The three adults looked at one another. "What do you mean, Danny?" his father asked.

"You know, Mr. Rogers from TV. Miss Sara gets to see him. Can I go, too?"

Dane dropped what he was holding and quickly moved

to the bed. He sat and pulled Danny onto his lap. "Tell me about Miss Sara going to see him," he said calmly.

Danny frowned. "Well, I hided behind Miss Sara's big suitcase, and that man came up to her. He told her that Mr. Rogers wanted to see her. I like Mr. Rogers, Daddy. I want to go see him, too."

Reagan's heart began to pound. Danny couldn't know that *Mr. Rogers from TV* had been dead for several years, and the man had to have been talking about another Mr. Rogers.

Reagan knew exactly who it was. And by the look on Dane's face, he knew it, too.

22

SARA

SARA WAS SO tired, and scared to the bone. She'd been up early that morning to catch her flight to Miami. She thought about everything she had been through over this long day. There was little chance that she'd make her flight to Orlando tomorrow morning. *There goes my second chance with Disney,* she thought. *And I'll never get a third.*

Would someone raise an alarm if she missed her flight? A sliver of hope needled its way into her heart. What would happen at Disney when she didn't show? Would Lance Petrie call Caitlyn? Just like that, her spirits fell. Probably not. He would be disgusted with Sara for not showing up and probably just dump her audition tape in the trash. And even if he did call them, none of her family knew that Sara had flown to Miami instead of Orlando. They'd think she was missing. Her stomach twisted painfully at the thought of causing them that kind of heartache.

What am I going to do? I have no way of getting out of here.

Sara looked around the room for the thousandth time. If she had to be a prisoner, she supposed this was better than any place she'd seen on TV where people were held hostage. By all accounts, this was an outrageously sumptuous hotel that catered to the ultra-rich. The room was decorated in gold and scarlet with its own fireplace. The sitting area was comprised of a large sofa and two elegant chairs. There was a desk at the other end of the room with a desktop computer and a credenza with a printer and some other equipment. The pictures on the walls and other accoutrements were tasteful and sophisticated. One entire wall was covered with gold and scarlet brocade draperies. Sara guessed that windows overlooking the ocean, and probably a balcony, were behind them.

Sara felt entirely out of her element. Her bodyguard sat stoically staring at her and only checked his phone occasionally. He ignored Sara when she asked his name.

She looked over at the glass-topped dining table at the congealed food in the wrapper that he had brought an hour ago. It was some kind of burrito, but Sara had only picked at it. Other than that, she'd only had a few sips of water.

The man's phone beeped, and he answered it. "Yeah?" He sat and listened. "Got it. Okay." He stuck the phone back in his pocket and looked at Sara. "Mr. Rogers can't get here tonight. He'll be here tomorrow."

"What does that mean?" Sara said.

"That means you stay here tonight." He stood and looked around, and his gaze settled on the bed. "You can sleep there. I'll be leaving soon and one of my associates will take my place."

Sara suppressed a shiver. She couldn't imagine being able to fall asleep with a strange man in the room.

As if he could read her thoughts, the man spoke. "It will be a woman."

"Oh." Sara nodded, and a wave of relief washed over her, although she still didn't think she'd be able to sleep.

"You have information that Mr. Rogers needs. Once you've answered his questions to his satisfaction, well then, he'll decide what to do with you."

Sara didn't like the sound of that. It almost sounded as if once she had imparted this information to Mr. Rogers, if she was no longer needed..." Sara forced herself to leave that train of thought.

It didn't matter anyway. Reagan might know the information Mr. Rogers wanted, but Reagan wasn't here, and Sara had no way of figuring out what it was, or of reaching her sister. What would Mr. Rogers do to her once he figured out that she wasn't Reagan?

Sara felt a tear slip out of one eye, and turned her head. She took a deep breath. *You can't cry. Reagan wouldn't cry.*

23

LATE WEDNESDAY NIGHT

DANE

DANE COULDN'T BELIEVE it. Reagan was right. Squeaky clean Florida Governor Rick Rogers was very likely involved—if not running—an operation to smuggle anti-cancer drugs into the US from Cuba in order to conduct illegal trials.

To her credit, she wasn't gloating. She understood the ramifications this would have on their state. She also understood that they still had a lot of work to do to find Sara and secure her safety, which was paramount.

Shane seemed to realize that something was seriously wrong, and had no doubt had guessed who "Mr. Rogers" really was. He moved alongside his brother. "How can I help?" he asked softly.

Dane was setting up his laptop. He glanced at Danny. "Keep him occupied, read to him, get him ready for bed. Reagan and I are going to have to leave soon."

Shane squeezed his shoulder. "I'm on it."

"You two will be safe here. Thanks." Dane jumped online as Reagan pulled up a chair next to his.

"Now what?" she said, her brow furrowed. "We still don't have any leads on where my sister is."

Dane nodded. "I know. But now we know that Rogers is up to his neck in this, and on his way here. So we let *him* lead us to her."

Reagan's eyebrows shot up. "Oh! You're right. That's brilliant. But what'll happen when he gets here? If he thinks she's me and starts asking her questions she can't answer? She might look like me, but she won't be able to hold her own with him."

Dane shook his head as he typed. "It won't get that far. We're going to find him, follow him to where they're holding her, formulate a rescue plan, create some kind of diversion to stall, and do a bait and switch."

"Bait and—? Oh, I get it," Reagan said. Her face lit up. She lowered her voice to a whisper. "Slip me in as Sara, she and I switch clothes, I put on the brunette wig, and I'm me again, and she gets out as herself. Oh my gosh, it might work."

"It *will* work," Dane said emphatically. "Oh, I thought of something else. We don't know for sure if she was wearing a wig under the baseball cap. Do you think she would have dyed her hair?"

Reagan shook her head vigorously. "Absolutely not. Her hair is her pride and joy. I'm sure it's a wig."

Dane felt a measure of relief. "Okay, good. That's one point in our favor." His fingers flew over the keys. "All you'll need to do is get Rogers on tape admitting to his part in the operation."

"On tape?"

"You'll wear a wire."

Reagan frowned. "What if they search me?"

Dane shrugged. "Why would they? They picked 'you' up in the airport. You've been their prisoner since." He leaned in and whispered even more softly. "*Sara* as you wouldn't have had any opportunity to get a tape recorder or anything out of her suitcase." Reagan nodded and he pointed to the screen.

"We need to track his texts and phone calls going back to noon today, from the time Sara landed in Miami—no, from when she hit the streets as you, this afternoon. Somebody had to have been assigned to watch for you. I'm sure they had your building and the *Herald's* office under surveillance. I can't figure out why they didn't take her in Miami. I mean, that would have been so much easier than letting her come here. It doesn't make any sense. And now, he has to come here, too." Dane frowned. "If he's on his way here, he won't fly commercial."

Reagan consulted her notes. "He won't come on one of the state planes," she murmured. "He'll make Navarro fly him here on one of his private jets. Yep, he has three of them. Do you have the call numbers?"

"I will, in about fifteen seconds," Dane said. He looked at Reagan. "Can you handle this? You remember how I showed you to get a data dump off a phone?" Dane went to the closet and dug around until he found what he was looking for.

"Sure. What are you doing?"

"Putting together our posse," he said with a smile. "We're going to need eyes and ears on the ground the minute Rogers hits Jardinian soil. I'm going to see Uncle Louie." He gave Danny a hug and kiss goodnight and headed out the door.

Dane quickly walked to the front lobby. It was time to come clean with Rose and Ike. His son and brother were here at the resort now and the owners had a right to know that. Dane would do his best to keep all the nefarious activity away from here, but nothing was guaranteed.

When he got to the lobby, Moni was sitting by herself, playing on her phone. She hopped up to greet Dane.

"Hello, sir Trey! Do you need some more help?"

"As a matter of fact, I do, Moni. I—ah, I need to talk with your Uncle Louie."

"I will take you to him!"

Dane smiled. "Great. But first, I need a minute with Rose and Ike." He didn't want to reveal his identity to Moni, yet. "I'll be right back."

He went to the front desk, where a young woman whose nametag said *Haley* greeted him. "May I help you?"

"Yes, I need to see Rose and Ike. It's important," Dane said.

"Sure, they're in their office," Haley said, pointing to a pink door across the lobby with a sign that read *Manager*.

The door was ajar. Dane knocked lightly and peeked in. "Hi, could I come in?"

"Of course!" Rose and Ike both stood to greet him. "How can we help you, Trey?"

Dane closed the door. "Well, I need your help, but first, I need to tell you who I really am." He opened his cred pack that he'd gotten out of the closet. "I'm Special Agent Dane Corsica with the DEA, based in Miami. I'm undercover on a case and needed a place to hide." He swallowed and leveled his most apologetic gaze on the elderly couple. "I didn't mean to deceive you, but it was an urgent matter," he said. "And I can assure you that no one here at the resort has ever been in danger," he added.

Rose and Ike exchanged a glance, and Rose took Dane's hand in both of hers. "And we assume that the young lady with you is not your wife."

Dane felt his face flush. He didn't want to reveal Reagan's identity just yet. "You're correct," he said. "She's a—a colleague, and we're not, you know, together, or anything. We're just here doing our jobs."

Ike patted Dane's arm. "You don't need to explain it to us, Dane," he said. "Or should we still call you Trey?"

"Yes, I think that'd be better until we get this wrapped up," Dane nodded.

"Well, Trey, sometimes these things work out," Rose said pleasantly. "You come to a romantic island like this, and suddenly, the one who's meant for you is at your side."

Dane resisted the urge to squirm. "Well, ah—I just need to get this case solved, and wanted to let you know that Moni is here to take me to her Uncle Louie. I need some local support, and I think he's the one to help me."

Rose and Ike both nodded vigorously. "Oh yes, Louie knows everyone on the island," Rose said.

"The little boy who was here earlier is my son, Danny."

"Oh yes, we know," Rose beamed up at him. "He has your eyes."

"Ah, well, thank you. My brother brought him here. They'll be staying in the room with—Sara, for the time being. I'll be glad to pay any extra charges for them being here, and of course, for their food."

Rose laid her hand on his shoulder. "Oh, don't worry a bit about that, Trey. Just go catch your bad guys!"

"And if we can help in any way, you let us know," Ike added.

24

REAGAN

PAY DIRT! REAGAN plugged in her ear buds and concentrated on the cell phone conversation between Governor Rogers and Doug Navarro that took place only a few hours ago.

"What happened? How did the St. Clair woman get past your guys?"

"I'm sorry, sir, they've been doing 24-hour surveillance for almost a week with absolutely no sign of her. She was already on the plane to St. Jardin before we could confirm the sighting. They just got sloppy."

"Sloppy is right. Fire all of them! I expect better from you, Navarro."

"I'm sorry, sir. I'll fix it—"

"No, you won't. I'm going to St. Jardin to talk to her myself. They got her at the airport, didn't they? You managed not to screw that up?"

"Yes, sir. We've got her at a hotel owned by a guy who we've done business with in St. Jardin.

"Who's that?"

"Bobby Olivier."

"Bobby O? Great. Another thug for me to run the chance of being seen with."

"He's out of the country, sir, so there's no chance of that. His hotel is at the north end of the island, very secluded, and they have a new wing they haven't opened yet. That's where we've stashed her. We can get you in and out of there without being seen."

"Well, that's the first thing you've gotten right."

"I have a jet standing by to take you to St. Jardin whenever you're ready, sir."

"Good. I'll let you know when I can get away. One more thing. Not one hair on her head is to be harmed, you got that?"

"Yes, sir."

"You make sure you communicate that to your people. Not one hair."

The call disconnected. Reagan's heart took wing. She knew where her sister was! And it looked like Sara wasn't in any imminent danger. She dialed Dane's burner phone and was relieved when he picked up. "I know where she is," she said in a rush. "It's a secluded hotel on the north end of the island. I'm sending you a text file of a conversation between Rogers and Navarro. And the best thing is—she's safe. They're not going to hurt her. Not unless they discover she's not me."

"That's fantastic," Dane said. "Moni and I are almost to the Boogie Shack. I'm going to talk with Uncle Louie and see what he knows about this hotel, and put together a plan."

"I have a few more things to follow up on," Reagan said.

"I wish I could figure out *why* Rogers is involved in this. It still doesn't sync up."

"Okay," Dane said. "Get ready to go. Bring my computer with you." Reagan heard Moni chattering in the background. "Moni will come back for you. Can you be ready in twenty minutes?"

"Yes," Reagan said. "I'll meet her out front. See you soon." Her mind was already leaping ahead. She just knew she could figure out why Rogers was involved. There had to be a compelling reason. All of this was completely out of character for him. It didn't sound like he and Navarro were partners, with Navarro calling him "sir" in every other sentence. The tone of both men's voices established Rogers as being in charge, and Navarro subservient, which had to be a new role for Navarro. Rogers was clearly disgusted at being associated with him.

Reagan closed her eyes and jumped when she felt a soft tap on her shoulder. She removed her ear buds and looked at Shane. "I'm sorry, I didn't mean to scare you," he said. "How's it going?"

"It's okay. Well, I'm making headway." She glanced over at the bed. "Is Danny asleep?"

Shane nodded and leaned against the back of one of the upholstered chairs, his long legs crossed at the ankles. "It's been a long couple of days for him." He fought a yawn and hooked his thumbs in his belt loops. "I may be joining him. Are you going to be leaving soon?"

Reagan nodded. She knew she could trust him. "I'm just missing one big piece of the puzzle, why Rogers has gotten involved with these reprehensible people. It's completely out of character for him. His whole career is at stake."

Shane looked deep in thought for a moment, and tilted his head at her. He stroked his chin with one hand. "Put yourself in his place. If you're a person with high moral character, what would make you do something that goes completely against your values? Or get involved with someone who you would *never* normally associate with?" His deep brown eyes bored into Reagan's. "What's the one thing that would drive you to risk your reputation and everything you've worked your whole life for?"

Reagan heard the faint sound of the ocean waves from the open patio door. As she stared at Shane, the answer suddenly became crystal clear. *"Family,"* she whispered.

Shane nodded.

Reagan's hands flew over the keys. She quickly navigated the back-door paths that Dane had shown her, and soon, she had her answer.

Rick Rogers' seventeen-year-old daughter, Jill, was battling cancer.

Reagan jumped up and before she knew what she was doing, she threw her arms around Shane's neck. "Thank you, Shane! Thank you so much!" Then she pulled back, moved her hands to rest on his shoulders, and realized that his were settled lightly around her waist.

He looked as flustered as she felt. "You're welcome, Reagan," he said softly.

They just stood there for a couple of seconds, but it felt much longer to Reagan, and she couldn't tear her eyes from his. Finally, she stepped back, and tucked a strand of hair behind her ear. "Well, I—um, I need to get going." Shane nodded silently.

Reagan ran into the bathroom, gathered her hair up into

a ponytail, and threw a few things into her purse. Then she went to her suitcase and retrieved something that was going to come in handy. She went back to the bedroom and pulled on her windbreaker, zipping it up.

She kept her eyes off Shane as she packed up the laptop and shoved it into its bag. "All right then, that's it," she said, looking around.

"You might need this," Shane said with a smile, reaching for her burner phone that was on the table.

Reagan blushed and held out her hand. "Thanks."

He held onto the phone. "How about I put my number in here? In case you need to get a hold of me."

Reagan nodded and reached for the phone when Shane held it out. Their fingers touched, and Reagan felt a tingle. *This is crazy. I mean, I thought maybe Dane and I....* She stepped away from Shane. She had to get a hold of herself. Sara was still out there under the control of Navarro's men, and even though things were looking up, it wasn't over yet. This wasn't the time to think about either of the Corsica brothers.

"Stay safe, Reagan," Shane said softly. "I'll be praying for you."

25

LATE WEDNESDAY NIGHT

DANE

BY THE TIME Moni dropped Dane off at the entrance to the Boogie Shack and roared off to retrieve Reagan, he'd read the text of the phone conversation and collected his thoughts. He entered the restaurant and gave his eyes a moment to adjust. Then he did a sweep and located Louie behind the bar.

The man grinned at him. "I knew you would be back! What'll it be? I will make for you the special of the day!"

Dane returned the smile. "I'm still going to have to take a raincheck on that. I'm here on business. Can we talk in private?"

Louie nodded and put down the glass he was drying. He gestured to a dark-haired youth working at the other end of the bar. "Amir! You're in charge." He gestured to Dane. "One of Moni's brothers. Come on."

Moni's brothers? Gustav, and now Amir? Dane glanced

139

over his shoulder at the young man. He looked kind of Middle Eastern. But Dane couldn't think about that now. He followed Louie through the saloon doors and through the busy kitchen into an office. Louie shut the door behind them, sat down at his desk, and indicated a chair for Dane.

"You FBI, CIA, or DEA?" Louie asked.

Dane looked at him evenly. "Who said I'm any of those?"

A slow grin took over Louie's tanned, weathered face. "I've been running this place for over thirty years, amigo. I know an American fed when I see one."

Dane didn't move for a second. Then he pulled his cred pack out of his waistband and flashed it. Louie nodded but didn't comment.

"The alias I'm using is Trey Armstrong," Dane said, putting the cred pack away. "That's how Moni knows me. I'd like to keep to that for a while."

"Fine," Louie said. "So, how can I help?"

"Do you know a hotel on the north end of the island owned by Bobby Olivier?"

Louie's eyebrows knit together, and he nodded. "Everyone in the Caribbean knows Bobby O. He's bad news. What business you have there?"

Dane quickly outlined what was going on. "An American—official is on his way here tonight or possibly tomorrow to meet with a reporter being held there in a new wing of the hotel that hasn't opened yet. That reporter is my partner, but it's her sister who was taken hostage through a mix-up. We need to get my partner in, and get the sister out, before the man arrives. I don't have any resources here, but you do."

Louie stroked his chin. "One of Moni's brothers works

there. Let me call him." He grabbed his cell phone and punched in a number.

Another brother? Dane thought. *Just how many are there?* His phone buzzed and he looked at the screen. It was from Reagan. *I have more info, and a plan. Moni and I need to make a stop. Be there in half an hour.* Dane squirmed in his seat. He needed to get his laptop set up to keep monitoring Navarro's and Rogers' conversations and/or texts to nail down precisely when Rogers would arrive on St. Jardin. His whole plan hinged on that.

"Fernando? You working tonight?" he heard Louie say. "Good. The family's gonna need some help later." He looked at Dane as he spoke. "I'll be in touch." He stood. "I just got a text from Moni. She be here in a while. Let me fix you the best drink in St. Jardin—no alcohol. You on duty."

Dane smiled and followed him back into the restaurant and sat at the bar, looking around at the authentic décor and the lights strung across the second-story balcony that looked over the main floor. "This is no shack, Louie," he said. "It's a great place."

Louie smiled and set Dane's drink in front of him. He gestured over his shoulder with a thumb. "The original shack is through there," he said with a broad smile. "It's our poker room now."

While Dane was waiting, he put the finishing touches on his plan. Even though Reagan said *she* had a plan, this was Dane's operation, and he would call the shots. He carefully walked through the steps to get Reagan in and get Sara out. He would need a few things to pull it off, but it would work. And, he'd need about a dozen strong, young men. He hoped Louie could corral together that many.

Dane took another sip of his delicious drink and heard a voice over his shoulder. "Good evening, Trey."

His eyebrows lifted. "Gustav, hello." The two shook hands, and Gustav swung up on an adjacent stool. "What brings you here?"

Gustav shrugged. "When Uncle Louie calls, I come." His eyes flicked over Dane's shoulder. "Ah—here are some more brothers. Meet Minh, Carlos, Nico, and Ray." Dane shook each hand as they smiled and nodded to him, and his confusion grew. This was an interesting family, to be sure. The four young men followed Gustav and sat down at a large, round table. It looked like a gathering of the UN.

Dane was thinking about joining them when Moni breezed in. "Hello, sir Trey!" she said, stopping to stand beside him. "You meet my brothers?" Dane nodded. "Hello, boys!" she said with a jaunty wave, and they all waved back and grinned at her.

Dane looked around. "Where's—um, Sara?" His eyes grew wide as Reagan followed her in. At least he thought it was Reagan. She was dressed in Sara's clothes, but wore her damp hair in a long, brunette braid. Dane blinked. He was so confused.

She stopped at his elbow. He looked into her eyes, and knew it was Reagan. "Yes, it's me. Moni and I stopped for hair dye. It's time to be me again."

Dane shook his head. This completely wrecked his plan. "What are you doing? How will we do the bait and switch?"

Reagan smiled. "We won't need to." She patted the laptop case that rested over one shoulder. "Can you and I go somewhere private?"

Dane stood, and looked around until he found Louie. "Louie, could we—"

"Of course. My office is yours."

Dane led Reagan through the kitchen to Louie's office and closed the door behind them. He put his hands on his hips. "I sure hope you know what you're doing, because you've completely shot my plan to—"

Reagan was already at Louie's desk, opening the laptop. "Dane, I have it all figured out. I know why Rogers is involved. One of his kids has cancer." She spoke with calm assurance.

Dane's mind went blank. "Which one?"

"Jill. She's seventeen."

It had been a long time since he'd seen the Rogers' three children. It must be the youngest one. Dane had a vague memory of a little girl with blond pigtails.

"He's contracted with Navarro to get the Cuban anti-cancer drugs to him in exchange for turning a blind eye to bringing them into the US to conduct illegal trials. And the drugs are working on his daughter—like *really* working. Rogers is risking everything, including his career and his freedom, to save his child's life."

Dane let the implications of that sink in. He sat at the computer and pulled up what he needed to do another data dump of Navarro's and Rogers' phones. He set it up so everything would come through as text on his screen in real time. As Reagan outlined her plan, he had to admit that it made sense.

"I know I can talk him down, Dane. Let me do this," Reagan begged.

"But we'll still need backup. You and I can't do it alone."

"Absolutely. We need a show of strength at the airport when his plane lands. And another group ready to go at the hotel."

Dane thought nervously about Moni's brothers and squeezed his eyes shut. A half-dozen young people wasn't much in the way of a show of strength. If this didn't work, he'd be the laughingstock of the DEA. He would probably need to start over somewhere else in a new career, something far removed from law enforcement.

There was nothing further on either Navarro's or Rogers' phones. Dane set an alarm to go off when something came in. He looked at Reagan's hopeful eyes. "All right, go get Moni. Tell her to bring Louie and her brothers in here."

Reagan quickly left and was gone for only a few seconds. When she came back, Dane was astonished when almost twenty people crowded into the room.

"Moni, how many brothers do you have?"

"Eleven. And five sisters," she said happily.

What? How is that possible? Dane couldn't believe it. He looked around the room filled with teens and early-twenty-somethings. The look on his face must have given him away.

"Oh! You think we are a regular family? Ha, ha. You are funny, sir Trey," Moni said. "Uncle Louie and Aunt Evie adopted us all. We're orphans. I love my family. You already know Gustav. This is Minh, Carlos, Nico, Ray, Mikhail, Amir, Tony, Heinrich, and Pierre. Our brother Fernando and sister Lucy work at Bobby O's hotel and are ready to do whatever you say." She nodded to the young women standing next to her. "And these are my sisters Carmen, Lily, Sabrina, and Kat. We are just as strong as our brothers. We want to help." The women smiled and nodded, just like Moni.

As he looked at the eager group, a thought hit Dane with the force of a sledgehammer. Rogers was willing to risk it all for his family. Reagan was like family to him, and Sara and the St. Clairs by extension. Families came in all shapes and sizes. Moni's unlikely group of brothers and sisters came tonight without question when Louie called.

An alarm went off on Dane's computer, and he and Reagan instantly looked at the screen. "They land at seven tomorrow morning," Dane said to the group. He looked at Reagan. "Go ahead, tell them the plan."

26

REAGAN

REAGAN STOOD ON the tarmac just outside one of the airport gates where private planes came in. Her windbreaker snapped in the early-morning breeze. To the east, fingers of rosy golden light crept into the indigo sky. But Reagan's gaze was focused to the west.

She looked at her phone, which read 7:07 a.m. *Come on, come on,* she coaxed, as if she could will the plane to get there any faster.

Reagan looked behind her through the floor-to-ceiling glass windows into the terminal where her team waited: five of Moni's brothers and two of her sisters, all dressed in dark clothing. It was all smoke and mirrors. They were supposed to look like a tactical team, and in the early-morning darkness, would probably pass muster. All of them had older rifles that Louie had produced back at the cantina just before they left, half of the group going with Reagan to the airport, the other half with Dane to the hotel.

But none of the weapons were loaded, except for Amir's. Reagan had no idea how Dane had gotten approval from airport management to even bring them on the property, but Louie had made a phone call and announced that everything was set. Reagan greatly admired him and was glad he was in their corner.

She kept her eyes trained on the western sky and suddenly, she saw the lights of a plane, and then she heard the smooth engines of the Gulfstream V as it grew closer in the sky. She turned and gave a thumbs-up to Amir, whom Dane had assigned as her team lead. Reagan walked forward on the tarmac as the group filed silently through the door and lined up in two perfectly straight lines behind her, standing at attention, their rifles at the ready.

The jet landed like a bird on a placid lake and rolled smoothly toward them, stopping in the middle of the tarmac. The engines powered down, and the forward door of the jet opened. A stairway glided noiselessly down to the pavement, and Reagan heard it lock in place.

This is it. Reagan took a deep breath and willed her heart to stay calm. *Lord, I know I haven't been good about staying in touch, but if you see me here, I'd appreciate your help, for Sara's sake. Amen.* It was the first prayer Reagan had prayed in years, and it should have felt awkward, but didn't.

A few short seconds later, she recognized the tall, athletic form of Rick Rogers as he appeared in the entryway and began to descend, alone. Reagan walked confidently to the bottom of the stairs and waited for him. As soon as he stepped onto the tarmac, she spoke. "Welcome to St. Jardin, Governor." She held up her press pass. "I'm Reagan St. Clair." She did not offer her hand.

Confusion knotted his features. "Reagan St. Clair? I don't understand."

"I'm sure you don't. You think I'm being held captive at the Golden Ruby Hotel. But as you can see, here I am, in the flesh." Rogers stuck his hands in his pockets as the wind whipped around them. Reagan looked straight into his eyes. "The woman at the hotel is my sister, Sara. Through a mix-up, Navarro's men grabbed her." Rogers' eyes grew wide. "Yes, I know your connection to Navarro. I also know about Jill." She clamped her lips shut to let that sink in.

Rogers hung his head, and then his Adam's apple bobbed as he swallowed. "Ms. St. Clair, I never meant for any of this to happen, for anyone to be harmed." Reagan watched his eyes fill. "I—my only intent was to save my daughter's life. I got in over my head."

Reagan recognized true contrition in the man's eyes, but her voice stayed hard. Her sister's survival depended on it. "You're going to do exactly as I say. I'm here with an armed squad authorized by the DEA." That of course wasn't true, but those were the exact words Dane had told her to say. "My partner is a senior DEA agent and is at the Golden Ruby with another armed squad. You're going to call Doug Navarro right here, right now, and tell him to call his men at the Golden Ruby and tell them to *stand down*, and immediately release my sister to my partner." She took out her cell. "I'm going to get on the line with him. Once I know my sister is safe, I'll take you to talk with my partner, and see what kind of deal he can make for you." Rogers didn't say anything.

Reagan pinned him with a hard stare. "If you don't comply with these orders," she said, looking over her shoulder, "you'll be taken into immediate custody and turned over to the DEA, and my partner and I will go straight to the prosecuting attorney and tell them everything we know. You're on foreign soil now, so this is a federal case. The DEA is outside Navarro's present location, front and back, right now. If he doesn't follow our orders, one call to them from my partner, and he'll be in cuffs in about ten seconds." Dane had assured Reagan that Navarro was going to be taken into custody either way, but Reagan wasn't going to tell Rogers that.

The governor nodded vigorously. He took out his phone. "Yes, of course, I'll—I'll make that call now."

Reagan activated her burner phone and called Dane. "Yeah?" he answered.

"He's calling Navarro now," Reagan whispered. She kept her eyes on Rogers.

"It's me," he said crisply into the phone. "I'm in St. Jardin. The woman at the Golden Ruby isn't Reagan St. Clair, it's her sister. Your guys screwed up *again*. You have to call them right now and tell them to release her. The DEA is here with me, and they're at the hotel waiting, and they're outside your place ready to take you into custody if you don't make the call." He took a breath. "*Do it now*, Navarro, or I swear I will use every resource at my disposal to hunt you down and you'll never see the outside of a cell." Rogers' voice shook and Reagan was mildly impressed by his intensity.

Rogers nodded to her, and Reagan whispered into the phone, "it's a go."

The next thing she heard was Dane shouting, "go, go, go!" and then the line went dead.

27

DANE

"GO, GO, GO!" Dane shouted. He shoved his phone in his pocket. The adrenaline flowed the way it always did during a raid, and he loved it. It didn't matter that he was with Moni and her ragtag family instead of a highly trained tactical team. After they had arrived at the Golden Ruby and gotten into place with the help of Fernando and Lucy, they had plenty of time while they waited for the call from Reagan. Dane versed his team in how things needed to go down—if Navarro's men complied, and if they didn't.

Now, they marched down the thickly carpeted hallway of the new wing. Dane was in front, followed by Gustav, who he'd designated as team lead, with the others in two flanks behind him. They were a little haphazard, but Dane felt in his gut that they would be sufficient. He rested his hand on the grip of a gun that Louie had given him, ready to pull it from its holster if needed. Only his and Gustav's weapons were loaded.

They reached the door to the suite where Sara was being held. The double doors stood open, and two muscular men stood on either side of it. When they saw Dane, they raised their hands. Dane glanced over his shoulder. "Take them into custody," he said to Gustav.

Dane rushed into the suite, with half of the team behind him, as planned. A female guard stood by the couch, her hands raised. "Cuff her," Dane ordered. Moni quickly moved to obey. "Secure the perimeter," he called out, and two of Moni's brothers carried out his orders exactly how he had instructed them.

"We're clear," they called back. Dane immediately pulled out his phone and got Reagan back on the line. His only concern was for Sara. She sat on the bed, her arms wrapped around her middle. Tears ran down her face. Dane flashed his cred pack at her and smiled. He felt like he already knew her. "Hi, Sara, I'm Special Agent Dane Corsica, DEA." He put his phone on speaker and held it out. "Go ahead, Reagan."

Reagan's voice shook as it came through loud and clear. "Peanut?"

"Reagan, is that you? I'm okay," Sara said with a sob. "Where are you?'

"Oh, thank God! I'm at the St. Jardin airport. I'll see you soon. Dane is—he's my best friend." Dane heard Reagan sniff. "He'll take good care of you. I love you, Sara."

"I love you, too, Reagan. I'm so sorry I got in the middle of this and messed everything up for you."

"Honey, none of this was your fault. It all worked out. We'll talk about it later. Dane, don't let her out of your sight."

"I won't, Reagan, I promise." He took the phone off speaker and held it to his ear. "Everything secure on your end?"

"Yes," Reagan said. "Rogers is ready to cooperate, completely."

Dane walked away to have some privacy, but didn't take his eyes off Sara. "I just got a text message from Miami. Navarro is in custody."

"Good. You did it, Dane! You got Navarro."

He smiled. "*We* got him. Couldn't have done it without you. And our team," he added.

Reagan laughed. "Our team! Who would have thought? Oh Dane, Moni took me to their—house to dye my hair. It's just a concrete building with two big dormitory rooms. I know Louie and his wife are doing everything they can, and it's more than a lot of people on the island have. It's so amazing that they've opened their hearts to these orphans, but I'm thinking we can help them—"

"We'll definitely make it happen, Reagan. Okay, we're going to lock everything down here. The St. Jardin police are going to take all these folks into custody, and I want to interview Rogers somewhere private, so let's meet up back at Rose and Ike's office." Dane had already called them and arranged this, and he gave Reagan further instructions. "Then you and Sara can get some sleep or go relax on the beach or something."

"Yes, I want to spend the whole day with her. See you soon."

Dane walked back over to Sara. He felt awkward towering over her, so he squatted down in front of her. "Are you okay? Can I get you anything?"

"I'm ready to be rid of this thing." She pulled off the brunette wig, the nylon cap came with it, and they fell to the floor. Her golden hair tumbled past her shoulders. Sara ran her fingers through the tangles and then swiped at her wet eyes. "Yes, I'm—I'm—" she began to shake. Tears poured out of her beautiful brown eyes, and Dane did the only thing he could think of to do.

He sat down next to her and opened his arms.

And Sara fell into them.

28

SARA

THE LAST TWELVE hours had been a nightmare, and it was finally over.

Sara was embarrassed that she couldn't stop crying, and that she'd flung herself into the handsome DEA agent's arms. Still, she hung on. It felt so good to have someone to lean on. For a moment, she tried to pretend that it was her dad or one of her brothers.

But being held by them had never felt like this.

Finally, she pulled back, and swiped at her face with her shirtsleeve. "I'm sorry," she whispered, her head down.

He didn't say anything, and after several seconds, his finger gently tipped her chin up. "You don't have anything to be sorry for." He wore a crooked smile that was very endearing, and his brown eyes searched hers. Something about him seemed a little familiar, but for the life of her, Sara couldn't figure out what it was.

She reached out and touched his shirtfront just below his shoulder. "Oh…I'm sorry. I got your shirt wet," she said with a grimace. Her face burned with embarrassment.

He laughed. "It's okay, Sara. Believe me, I've had *much* worse happen to me. Are you okay staying here a little while longer? I can't leave until the police arrive."

Sara blew out a breath. "Yes, I'm fine. I'd like to go wash my face."

He stood. "Let's go." Sara's eyes widened. "Hey, I promised Reagan I wouldn't let you out of my sight." He gave her a full-on grin now, and Sara felt her heart trip. She crossed the room to the elegant bathroom and let the cool water sluice over her tear-stained face. It felt wonderful. In the mirror, she saw the DEA agent leaning against the door jamb, his arms crossed in front of him.

She dried her face and turned to face him. "I'm sorry, what was your name again?"

"Dane."

Dane. It fit him perfectly. Sara smiled at him. "I'm sure my sister would let you off the hook to let me use the bathroom."

Dane grinned and started to pull the door closed. "I'll be waiting."

As soon as it clicked shut, Sara put her hands to her cheeks, which had suddenly grown warm again. *Gosh, he's so attractive.* She finished her business, washed her hands, and tried to finger-comb her hair. "It's a lost cause," she muttered to herself. She took a breath and opened the door. He was standing right where she'd left him.

"Hi," she said a little breathlessly. She didn't mean for it to come out that way, and wanted to kick herself. *He'll think you're fourteen.*

Dane gave her that crooked grin again. "Hi." He uncrossed his arms and slid his hands in his pockets. "I'm sorry we have to stay here in this room. It's probably the last place you want to be. Do you want to sit down?"

Sara shook her head. "It feels good to stretch my legs." They walked back into the main room.

Dane looked at the wall covered in rich draperies and walked toward it. "I think there's a balcony behind these drapes somewhere." He went to the far right and found a panel of buttons on the wall. He pressed one, then another, and different parts of the drapery parted. It appeared that the entire wall was floor-to-ceiling glass. "Wow, that's pretty cool," he said with a sparkling smile. "My apartment sure doesn't have anything like that."

The balcony faced north to the ocean, and the sun was streaming through. He opened the sliding-glass door and motioned for Sara to go through. She went to the railing and leaned on it. As far as she could see, the ocean waters sparkled under the morning sun, every hue of blue and teal imaginable.

"It's gorgeous," she murmured.

"Yes, gorgeous," Dane echoed. Sara glanced at him, and he was staring at her. He looked away, and so did she.

"I don't see many beaches in the Midwest," Sara admitted. "Well, Lake Michigan. But it doesn't look like this."

"I'm from Florida," Dane said. His eyes were on the ocean view now. "I never get tired of it."

They stood there for a long time, drinking in the beauty of the morning. The rhythmic crashing of the waves was like a soothing balm. She liked that Dane seemed content to just be there with her.

"How long have you known Reagan?" she asked.

"About four years. We work together on cases sometimes. She's a good investigative reporter."

Sara nodded. "I know, but I worry about her. She doesn't have much of a life outside of work."

Dane smiled. "That may be about to change." Sara was going to ask what he meant by that when his phone rang. "Hold on." He listened for a moment. "That works. I'll touch base with your officers when they get here, and then wait for you. Thank you." He turned to Sara. "That was the Chief of Police. He's coming personally to oversee the transfer of these folks into custody, but he won't be here for about an hour, and he needs me here. Do you mind waiting until I can leave and take you to Reagan?"

Not if I can pass the time with you, Sara thought. "I don't mind at all."

"I'll be right back."

Sara stared out at the mesmerizing ocean again. Her flight to Orlando had already left, and since she didn't have her phone and it was likely dead by now, she had no way of getting a hold of Lance. Her second chance with Disney had slipped through her fingers, and she knew she'd never get another. It should have upset her more than it did. For some reason, Sara felt that this was all a part of God's plan.

She heard voices and turned her head toward them. Four local officers had just arrived, and they all shook hands with Dane and his second-in-command. After a few moments, Dane came back to the balcony.

"They have everything under control," he said. "How about you and I go get some breakfast? Or at least some coffee?"

Sara looked back toward the beach, which was quickly

becoming awash in the golden morning light. "You know what I'd really like? A walk along the beach."

Dane's face lit up. "That's a great idea. Come on." He laid his hand lightly on her arm, and they went back through the room. "We'll be back," Dane said to the group. He spoke to the tall, dark blond man. "Gustav, call me if you need me."

Sara followed Dane into the hallway. It felt good to be out of that room. He looked both ways. "Let's go left," he said. "There's probably a stairwell at the end of the hallway."

He was right, and he opened the door for her that led into the stairwell. When it closed behind them, it was completely dark, but Sara felt safe with him. "Wow, they must not have the lights installed yet. This whole wing is brand new, still under construction," he said by way of explanation. He clicked the light on his phone and a small puddle of light appeared in front of them. "You ready?"

"Yes," Sara nodded.

"Here, take my hand," Dane said. Sara laid her left hand in his right, and by some unspoken agreement, they laced their fingers together.

And then it happened.

29

DANE

DANE'S HEART BEGAN to thunder, and his breath caught in his throat. He looked at Sara, and knew she felt it, too.

He felt his face break into a grin, and she smiled back. Dane had an irresistible urge to sweep her into his arms, but something held him back. He held his phone out in front of him, shining the light on the stairs as they descended.

Holding Reagan's hand hadn't felt like this, and Dane couldn't remember much about the good times with Sally Ann, the early days of which were buried under an alcohol-induced fog.

They got down the three flights of stairs, and Dane wished it was three hundred. The zinging from their clasped hands raced up his arm, and he felt like he was holding one of those fourth-of-July sparklers.

They reached the bottom stair, and a closed door. Dane figured it led into a hallway, but didn't know if it was in a construction area or if it would be filled with people. He reluctantly let go of Sara's hand. "Hold on, let me look," he said softly. He carefully pulled the door open and peeked out. To the right was a hallway that looked like it might lead to a lobby area. Immediately to the left was a glass door leading outside.

He opened the door wider, pointed left, and ushered Sara through. He hung back for a moment, and then joined her in the early-morning tropical breeze.

Sara lifted her face to the sun, lifted her arms, and spun around. "Oh, this feels fantastic!" she said with a laugh. Then she stopped. "You probably think I'm crazy."

Dane thought his smile might split his face open. He could have stood there all day watching her. "No, I don't. You're not crazy at all." He laughed. "Come on, let's go!" He started jogging through the grass toward the shoreline and she trotted alongside. The grounds of the hotel were actually on a rise above the ocean. When they reached the rocky edge, Dane could tell it was an easy enough jump down. "I'll go first," he said. As soon as he landed on the sand, he turned around and held his arms out for her. She put her hands on his shoulders and he easily lifted her to the ground.

And time stood still. He didn't want to let her go.

Finally, she lowered her hands. They quickly shed their footwear, rolled their jeans up, and went to the water's edge. Sara squealed when the first wave cascaded over her feet. Her eyes sparkled at Dane. "Oh, this is heavenly!"

This is *heaven,* Dane thought. They began to walk along the sand, laughing and talking. Once when Sara ventured out a little, a wave knocked her off balance, and Dane caught her, which made them both laugh even more. He wanted to hold on to her, but held himself in check.

They kept walking until Dane looked at his phone and decided they should go back.

"You're with the DEA, so is this whole thing about a drug case?" Sara asked.

He nodded. "Reagan and I were both working the case undercover from different points, and ended up at a meeting together. We met up later to compare notes, and someone shot at us. They didn't hit us," he was quick to reassure her. "So basically we went on the run and needed a place to hide, and ended up here."

Sara didn't say anything for a few moments. "A little while ago, you said her life outside work might be about to change." She looked up at him expectantly. They were back to where they'd left their shoes, and put them back on. Then Dane looked around and spied a sort of rocky path where they could climb back up to the hotel grounds.

When they got back on even footing, he looked at Sara and shrugged. "My brother ended up coming here, and I think they kind of hit it off."

Sara looked at him incredulously. "Reagan hasn't been interested in a man in…forever." They were back at the door now. She grabbed his arm. "Dane! What if it's locked?"

He couldn't hold back his grin. He opened the door and peeled off the little piece of adhesive that he carried in his wallet for times like this.

Her beautiful brown eyes went wide, and she gasped. "Just like James Bond!"

Dane laughed and swore his chest expanded six inches. He took her hand and opened the door to the stairwell. "Come on, let's go."

30

SARA

WHEN THEY GOT back to the room, Sara lowered herself into a deep scarlet silk chair and watched Dane greet the police chief of St. Jardin and the other officers. It was clear that he was in command, yet respectful of everyone else around him. The officers got the three guards secured with their own handcuffs and returned the other ones to the people who were with Dane. They seemed a little scruffy and she supposed they were undercover operatives.

Sara couldn't keep her eyes off Dane. It felt like there were a thousand butterflies in her stomach. She still couldn't shake the sense of why he seemed familiar to her. There was no doubt in her mind that some of his interaction with her was pure flirting, but it was different—not like the way the college guys flirted, for no reason or just to see how far they could get with a girl. When his fingers had slipped through hers at the top of the stairs, and their palms met, Sara felt little electric shocks all the way up her arm, and she knew he felt the connection, too.

She couldn't believe how much fun she had walking and talking and laughing with him. He seemed incredibly mature, but of course that made sense. For someone with a successful career in the DEA, he had to be several years older than her.

He lived in Miami, which would make having a relationship impossible. Sara's head was swimming. She had never thought about leaving the Midwest. Could she live in Florida? She gave herself a shake. *Stop. You're moving too fast.*

She stood, and Dane's eyes connected with hers. She wordlessly pointed toward the bathroom and could tell he got the message.

As she stood at the sink washing her hands, Sara looked at her reflection. Even though she was exhausted both physically and mentally, her eyes looked bright and her cheeks were flushed. Dane's handsome face filled her mind. *After today, you'll probably never see him again.* Her heart deflated like a balloon.

She went back into the room and curled up in one corner of the couch, and promptly fell asleep. She dreamed of walking on the beach with Dane hand-in-hand at sunset, and of a glorious, romantic kiss.

31

DANE

THE PAPERWORK WAS signed, the prisoners were gone, and Fernando and Lucy had assured Dane that they would put the suite back in order. He shook everyone else's hand and promised to catch up with them later. He wanted to talk with Reagan and figure out a way to show their appreciation to their "team."

He'd been up all night, but had a lot to do before he could sleep. First, he had to interview Rick Rogers. That was going to be an uncomfortable conversation, but Dane was a professional and was confident he could handle it. He was certain someone much higher on the chain of command would make the recommendation about whether and how to charge the governor.

Then he would need to get back on grid with the DEA, complete reports, and make sure everything was wrapped up with Navarro's gang. Dane didn't want any procedural slip-ups that would jeopardize their case when it went to trial.

He knew this case would be a huge feather in his cap,

and in Reagan's. It was already early in his career to be a special agent, and this would most assuredly propel him to the next level. Right now, his head should be filled with the possibilities on the horizon for his career.

But he couldn't think about any of that now, because his mind was filled with Sara.

She completely captivated him. Holding her had brought out every protective instinct in Dane, and when she slipped her soft, feminine hand into his, he felt fireworks exploding in his hand up to his heart. He could have walked on the beach with her for hours, just communing with nature and engaging in easy conversation. He couldn't wait to spend more time with her.

The officer who introduced himself as Sergeant Aubert was going to drive them to the resort in a cruiser. Everyone else had left. Dane walked over to where Sara was sitting and realized that she'd fallen asleep. Whatever she was dreaming about brought a beautiful smile to her heart-shaped face, and he wished he could kiss her awake.

He gently shook her shoulder. "Sara," he said softly.

She opened her eyes and blinked, then yawned. "Oh gosh, I feel asleep."

"I'm sure you're exhausted. I'll take you to Reagan now. She's out at a resort where we're been staying."

The moment her hand touched his, the zinging started again. She smiled as she rose. "Oh, good. There are my bags."

"I'll get them," Dane said. He went to grab a handle with each hand to set them upright, and they almost pulled him off his feet. "Wow—what do you have in here?" he exclaimed with a laugh.

Sara turned pink and giggled. "Oh—just mostly—well, everything I own."

Dane got one bag up and Aubert, the other one. "At least I won't have to go to the gym today," the sergeant said under his breath. He and Dane both stifled a laugh.

They got down to the hotel entrance, and the brawny man deposited the baggage into the trunk of the cruiser. Dane held the passenger door for Sara, and she climbed into the backseat. He wished he could sit back there with her, but didn't want to make Aubert feel like a chauffeur.

It took about forty minutes to get to the resort, and the time passed quickly as the sergeant pointed out landmarks and answered Sara's enthusiastic questions.

Dane texted Reagan when they were almost to the resort, and she was standing at the front door when they pulled into the circular drive. As soon as the car came to a stop, Dane got out and opened Sara's door. She ran straight into Reagan's arms, and they stood there clinging to one another, rocking back and forth.

Dane and Aubert lifted Sara's bags out of the cruiser and Dane shook his hand and thanked him for his help. As the car drove away, he turned back to look at the two women, who were now arm-in-arm, smiling and drying their tears. "Wow," he said. "Seeing the two of you together—really, if it wasn't for the hair color, the resemblance is uncanny."

They looked at one another and laughed. "It's pretty weird," Reagan said. "You saw how much Landon and Brandon look alike, too. But they don't look like us."

"He met them? When?" Sara looked surprised.

"Right after Brandon and Morgan's wedding," Dane said.

Sara narrowed her eyes at her sister. "Yeah, I heard you were there." She looked between them. "I need to hear the whole story sometime."

Dane recalled the image that was burned into his memory of Sara at the wedding in her flowered sundress, talking and laughing with the other guests. The first time he'd laid eyes on her.

"I know I have a lot of explaining to do, and we'll get to that." Reagan said. She started to pull Sara toward the garden path. "Are you hungry? They're still serving breakfast on the patio."

Sara nodded. "Yes. I really haven't eaten much since yesterday afternoon."

"I'll get your bags upstairs," Dane said. Sara and Reagan began to walk away, chattering.

Suddenly, Reagan stopped and turned around. "What am I thinking?" she exclaimed, and ran to Dane. She threw her arms around his neck and almost knocked him over. "Thank you so much for rescuing my sister!"

32

SARA

SARA STOOD AWKWARDLY while Reagan and Dane embraced. His laughter floated through the air, and his arms came firmly around her sister. Something on his left hand glinted in the sun, and Sara couldn't believe her eyes. He was wearing a wedding ring! *Married? He's married? How is that possible? How did I not see that before?* Her heart jumped into her throat, and she felt her stomach plummet to her feet.

Reagan skittered back and looped her arm through Sara's, and Dane left with Sara's luggage. "Come on, let's go. The food here is out of this world," her sister said.

Sara's appetite had vanished. Now she just wanted to go curl up in a ball and cry her eyes out. What Dane must think of her, acting like an adolescent girl while he flirted with her and held her hand! Suddenly, her heartbreak turned to anger. *What a slimeball!* How could she have been so naïve and trusting? Sara took a deep breath and swallowed the bitterness down. She didn't want Reagan to start asking questions.

"Wait!" Reagan exclaimed. "Aren't you flying to Orlando this morning?"

Sara shook her head. "I missed my flight. I guess it wasn't meant to be. Again."

"Peanut, I'm so sorry. Are you sure? Have you called them? I could talk with them, tell them what happened—"

"No, I got my phone back, but it's dead and until I can charge it, I don't have any way to reach them." Sara wasn't ready to tell Reagan that she had a very strong sense that she wasn't supposed to go to Orlando. She was still trying to figure that out in her own mind. Suddenly, it was all too much. She swiped at a tear. "I just—I just want to be with my sister right now."

Reagan wrapped her arms around Sara. "I called Landon to let him know you're safe."

"Was he mad?"

Reagan pulled back and looked confused. "He was relieved. Why would he be mad?"

Sara looked down. "Because I took off on my own and didn't tell anyone where I was going. And I concocted this stupid plan to try to get my passport back." She clamped her teeth over her lower lip. "Do Mom and Dad know about any of this?"

"No. Just us four kids and Kelsea and Morgan." She looked into Sara's eyes. "You're not to blame for any of this. You had no way of knowing that I was being watched. If anyone is to blame, it's Dane and me for agreeing to the plan for me to travel on your passport without telling you."

"Was it your idea, or his?"

Reagan started walking. "It was actually Brandon's, at first. But Landon put all the wheels in motion." Sara nodded. That's what Landon did. But she was still annoyed at her siblings for not including her, not giving her adult status.

The sisters arrived at the patio. "I'll tell you about it later." Reagan's eyes lit up. "Oh good, there's Shane."

Shane? Sara followed Reagan's gaze to a corner table, and felt the blood drain from her face. It was Danny and his dad! What were they doing here? How did Reagan know them?

Danny looked up as they approached. "Miss Sara!" the little boy squealed. Sara thought he must be looking at Reagan, since the "Miss Sara" he sat with on the plane had a dark braid, but instead, he ran straight to her. She bent down and scooped him up.

"Danny, hi! How did you know it was me, since I looked like her on the airplane?" She pointed to Reagan.

"I just knew it was you, Miss Sara," he said, and threw his arms around her neck.

Shane was staring at Reagan, and then his gaze flicked to Sara. "I'll bet you're surprised to see us." He held out his hand. "I'm Shane Corsica."

"Oh..." Sara nodded. *Dane's brother! That explains a lot.* As she shook his hand, she tilted her head at Reagan. "Shane and Dane?"

Reagan and Shane laughed and shook their heads. "Yeah, we think it's hilarious, too," Reagan said. Her eyes were bright and her face a little flushed. Sara glanced at Shane, whose attention was entirely on her sister. *Well, it looks like Dane was right.*

Reagan looked between Shane and Sara. "Didn't you two meet on the plane?"

Shane smiled at Sara. "Well, ah—Sara and Danny got around to names, but we didn't."

Danny laid his head on her shoulder. "I'm so happy you came here, Miss Sara. I missed you."

Sara's heart swelled. "Aww, I missed you, too, Danny."

"Hey, everyone," Dane's voice came from behind Sara, and she felt herself stiffen.

Danny began to wiggle, and Sara set him down. "Daddy, Daddy!" he squealed, and launched himself into Dane's arms. Sara's eyes went wide. *What in the world?*

Sara looked at Shane in confusion. "You mean, you're not—"

"Oh, no. I'm not his dad. I'm his uncle. I was bringing him here, to Dane." *Good heavens, he's not just married, he's a father. Unbelievable.*

Danny bounced in his dad's arms. "Daddy, Daddy, Miss Sara's here!"

"I know," Dane said. "I'm glad that makes you happy. It makes me happy, too." He looked straight at Sara as he said it, and she forced herself to hold his gaze with the iciest one she could conjure up. She hoped he got her message.

Sara tapped her sister's arm. She wanted to get away from Dane. "Reagan, can we get some food now?" It looked as if Shane and Danny had already eaten.

"Yes, yes, of course," Reagan said. "Let's go."

"Where's Rogers?" Dane asked Reagan. Sara was glad that he seemed to be avoiding looking at her. He set Danny down and the little boy ran back to where he'd been sitting.

"In a small conference room off the lobby, thanks to Rose and Ike." She pulled a cell phone out of her pocket and handed it to him. "I took his phone. He can't contact anyone.

Amir is standing guard outside the door until you get there, just like you asked."

"Good work," Dane said, and squeezed her shoulder. "I'm off to interview him." He looked at his brother and tipped his head at Danny. "Do you mind?"

"No, not at all," Shane responded.

"Thanks. Did you eat all your breakfast, buddy?"

Danny kept coloring, and Shane spoke up. "He ate a banana and half of his pancakes. And all his milk."

Dane gave his son a thumbs-up. "That's good. See you guys later."

"What about breakfast?" Reagan asked. "You haven't eaten, either."

He waved a hand as he walked away. "Later. I'll grab some coffee in the lobby."

Sara went with Reagan to the buffet. She was glad to get away from the Corsica brothers. They were entirely too...distracting. She felt oddly drawn to both of them, which was totally unlike her. Shane was too old, and seemed enamored of Reagan. Dane was far more handsome, in Sara's opinion, but he'd shown his true character and even if by some strange turn of events he became available someday, she wanted nothing to do with a man like that. She tried to put him out of her mind as she filled a plate with scrambled eggs, an English muffin, and fruit.

When they got back to the table, Reagan sat down next to Shane, and Danny looked up from his coloring. "Sit by me, Miss Sara."

"Please," his uncle prodded.

Danny looked at Sara with an impish smile. "Please, Miss Sara."

Sara's heart melted. She would do anything for this little guy. But where was his mother? The one who'd put the gold wedding band on Dane's finger?

33

REAGAN

AFTER BREAKFAST, REAGAN, Sara, Shane, and Danny went to the lobby. Reagan wanted to check on Dane's progress with Rogers. She saw him coming out of a room, and crossed to him. He closed the door behind him and nodded to Amir. "Two DEA agents are coming within the hour to take him back to Florida," he said. "I'll be around until they arrive to sign off on the transfer."

"I will stay here as long as you need me, sir," Amir said formally.

"Thanks." Dane shook his hand. He led Reagan back to where Sara and Shane stood. "Well, I'm done with that."

"Done? I thought we were going to interview him together," Reagan said.

"Nope. DEA business only. No reporters allowed," he said with a wink.

Reagan crossed her arms in front of her. "I can't believe it. I'm the one who figured everything out. You're really going to freeze me out?"

Dane looped a friendly arm around her shoulder. "I

know, and the DEA appreciates it. And you'll get the exclusive. How's that?"

Reagan uncrossed her arms. "That's more like it, Corsica," she answered.

Dane turned and looked at Sara tentatively. "Maybe we could all do something this afternoon," he said, including Reagan and Shane. But it looked to Reagan that he only had eyes for Sara.

Sara crossed her arms in front of her chest. "No, count me out," she said. She gave no explanation, but her voice could have bent nails. Reagan frowned. *What in the world is wrong with her?*

"Good morning!" a voice trilled. Here came Rose, with Ike trailing behind her. Reagan and Dane exchanged a glance. They knew they had some explaining to do.

"Good morning," they said in unison.

Rose laid her hand affectionately on Dane's arm and looked up at him. "Did you catch your bad guys?"

Dane laughed. "We sure did, Rose." He nodded to both of them. "Thank you so much for your help."

"Oh, we didn't do anything," Ike said. "Just provided a place for you to grill your suspect. Is that what he is?"

"More or less," Dane said. "We should wrap things up there pretty soon and be out of your hair."

"Oh, it's no problem at all," Rose said. "So, what are you calling yourself now, Trey or Dane?"

Dane smiled, "I'm back to Dane, and staying there."

Rose looked at Shane. "This must be your brother."

"Yes," Dane said, and made the introductions.

"Thank you for letting us stay here," Shane said. "This is a beautiful resort."

"We're happy to have you," Rose said.

Ike looked at Sara. "And who is this pretty young lady?" Reagan hadn't noticed that Sara was hanging back behind her.

"Oh." Dane's mouth opened, and he and Reagan exchanged another glance. Sara looked at her sister expectantly.

"Well," Reagan began, "this is actually my sister. It's kind of a complicated story." She wasn't looking forward to untangling it. "Her name is Sara. I kind of—borrowed it."

"We know," Rose said brightly. "She's Sara St. Clair, and you're Reagan."

Dane and Reagan's jaws dropped in sync. Dane's eyes narrowed. "How did you know?"

Rose sniffed. "My dear boy, we knew as soon as we met your wife. After all, Landon was the one who called and arranged for you to come here. Oh, he didn't say a thing, but it was obvious to us, wasn't it, Ike?" Her husband nodded.

Sara looked between Dane and Reagan and speared her sister with a look. "Wife? Wait—you and he—are married?"

"Oh no, they're not even in love," Rose said emphatically. "You weren't very convincing," she muttered.

Dane's face turned red, and Reagan wished the ground would swallow her up. She couldn't bring herself to look at Shane. "No, we're not," Reagan said, swallowing a laugh. Rose was just too much. "We just—we came here to hide, and since this is a honeymoon resort, we had to go undercover as a newlywed couple." Reagan glanced at Sara, who looked positively furious. Reagan could read her sister's mind as if she'd shouted it: *just how "undercover" did this thing get??* "So of course, we—we had to stay in the same room," she went on, "but we didn't—ah—" *Oh dear. Why did I go down this path?*

"Reagan had rules," Dane interrupted. His voice cracked on the last word, and he looked like he was trying not to laugh. "There was a pile of pillows down the middle of the—" Dane glanced at Danny. "You know, like a concrete barrier." Reagan wondered if the little boy was understanding any of this.

"Daddy, can we go look for seashells?" Danny asked innocently. Relief stole over Dane's features. He leaned down and touched his son's red hair.

"I can go in a little while. I have to wait for some friends to come."

"I'll take him," Shane offered. "You can catch up." Reagan admired his easygoing way with his nephew.

"Thanks, that'd be great," Dane replied.

One of the resort's employees approached Rose and Ike with a question, and they left with a promise to see everyone later. "Head west when you get to the beach," Ike said to Shane. "That's where the best shells are."

"Miss Sara, will you come look for seashells with us?" Danny said. The little guy sure had attached to her. Reagan knew she was exhausted and was surprised at her response.

Sara still looked tense, but smiled at Danny. "Sure, I'd love to see the beach. I just need to go upstairs and change. I've been in these clothes for almost twenty-four hours."

"I'll go with you," Reagan said. Her words were directed at Sara, but she was looking at Shane.

"Um, Sara, could we talk for a moment?" Dane asked.

What was going on with the two of them? Dane looked miserable, and her sister looked like she was about to blow a gasket.

Sara didn't say anything for several seconds. Then she spoke a single, terse syllable. "Sure." They walked over by the stairs and began a whispered conversation. Sara had her back to Reagan and Shane, but Dane was visible in profile. Reagan could tell by their body language that Dane was trying to be agreeable and Sara definitely was not.

Reagan moved to stand next to Shane. "Do you know what this is about?" she whispered. He shook his head. Then Sara abruptly turned and marched up the stairs. Anger punctuated every one of her staccato footfalls.

34

DANE

WELL, SO MUCH for that. His heart felt like it had been torn out of his chest, stomped on, and stuffed back in.

He stuck his hands in his pockets and ambled over to his brother and Reagan.

"What's up with you and Sara?" Reagan asked.

Dane shook his head. "Ask her," he said tersely.

He saw a look pass between Reagan and Shane. "I'll be down in a few minutes," Reagan said.

Shane waited until she was out of earshot. "What's up?" he asked.

Dane didn't say anything for a moment. "I don't understand women."

Shane threw back his head and laughed. He laid his hand on Dane's shoulder. "Said every man who ever walked the earth." He squeezed Dane's shoulder. "I'm sorry."

Dane looked at his brother, who was watching Reagan go up the stairs. He recognized that *take no prisoners* look in Shane's eye.

"You're going to go after her," he said.

Dane expected Shane's face to break out in a grin, but he looked serious. "You bet I am." Shane crossed his arms in front of him and leaned against the back of a couch, crossing his feet at the ankles. "She's the one I've been looking for all my life. I could never put it into words, but I've always been certain that when I found her, I'd know. Make sense?"

Dane nodded. "Completely." He shook his head. "I've known her for a few years. You've got your work cut out for you."

Now the smile that Dane was expecting came, and Shane rested his hands on his thighs. "No, this is God's work." Then his countenance got serious again. "You know I would never marry a woman who didn't love God more than she loved me. Reagan needs to find her way back to Him first. I'm going to stick by her every step of the way, and be there with open arms when she arrives."

Dane couldn't believe that just a little while ago, he was trying to figure out how to work a long-distance relationship with Sara. "Well, at least you're both from Miami. Maybe you can ask her out when you get home."

Shane shook his head and smiled. "You've been with Reagan in disguise for too long. Come on, you know that won't work. We had an opportunity to talk for a long time this morning while we were waiting for you and Sara to get here, but even before that, I invited her to come tour the Miracle Center, and she accepted."

"Nice," Dane said with a grin.

Shane stood and clapped a hand on Dane's shoulder. "Is there anything I need to know about...well, about your *pretend* marriage? Let's clear the air now."

Dane shook his head and made an X on his chest with his finger. "Just one tiny kiss on the cheek. There was a little spark there, but only when she looked and acted like—well, Sara."

Shane grinned, and then his expression grew serious. "What's going on with you two?"

Dane blew out a breath. "Well, there was this, like, instantaneous combustion when we met. Like, sparks *everywhere*. I wasn't sure if it was because I rode in on my white horse and rescued her, but man, it was something else. We spent a couple of *incredible* hours together this morning. I thought there was real potential for it to go somewhere. And then suddenly, after we got here, she went as cold as an iceberg. Just now, she thanked me for rescuing her, and then said goodbye. I asked her what happened earlier today, and she said that it was a mistake and to leave her alone. And then she walked off."

"I think she's attracted to you," Shane said. "But she's fighting it. Want to hear my theory?" he grinned.

"Do I have a choice?" Dane muttered.

Shane ticked his points off on his fingers as he spoke. "First, she didn't realize you had a child. Second, she thought you were married to her sister. Third, because you have a child, even though you're *not* married to her sister, now she thinks you're married to someone else, because you're wearing a ring." He pointed at Dane's hand.

Dane looked down at the gold band, and wanted to kick himself. *Why didn't I realize that Sara would have noticed it?* "I put my ring in a drawer when Sally Ann left me for good. But when I started wearing this one for this assignment, I didn't even think about it." He slowly twisted it off and dropped it in his pocket. "You got all that from watching Sara for, what? A few minutes? You're crazy." His mind spun with the implications. Could his brother be right?

Shane shrugged and smiled. "I've been told I'm especially perceptive when it comes to people.

And I've never seen you look at a woman like you look at her."

Danny was sitting on a couch over the by the window, looking out at the garden and singing to himself. Dane lowered his voice. "I've only been a widower for two days."

Shane clapped a hand on his shoulder. "Legally, yes, but that marriage was over a long time ago." He squeezed. "I know you had your reasons for not ending it, and even though you took the ring off, you honored those vows, even when your wife probably didn't." His eyes were serious. "I respect you tremendously for that. Ninety-nine-point-nine percent of men wouldn't." Dane let that sink in. "God just may be rewarding your faithfulness. He's literally dropped a beautiful Christian woman in your path. The timing is aggressive, to be sure, but God's ways are not our ways. She and Danny are already crazy about each other."

Dane sighed. "You're serious, aren't you?"

Shane nodded. "I've seen stranger things."

"Tell me the truth, Shane. Was there a spark between you and Sara, even a tiny one, when you first met?"

Shane smiled and held his thumb and forefinger a little ways apart. "About this much, when I thought she was Reagan." They both laughed. Shane shook his head. "Sara's too young for me, and too sweet."

"I like sweet," Dane admitted.

Shane made a face. "I can take it, but only in small doses."

Dane laughed. "Then you're definitely going for the right woman."

Danny came bouncing over to them. "Can we go, Unca Shane?"

Shane stood. "Sure can." He looked at his brother. "Maybe Reagan will straighten her out, and then you can talk again."

Dane saw two DEA agents entering the front door. He'd try to figure out how to fix things with Sara later. "I can't think about that right now, Shane. I have a job to do."

35

SARA

SARA TOOK A deep breath and filled her lungs with the salt air. The beach was gorgeous, and what little of the gardens she'd seen were incredible. She wiggled her toes in the pristine white sand. Every shade of blue and aqua surrounded them. The golden sun smiled down on her, and with every breath she took, she felt the tension ebbing away. There was a unique, sweet scent to the tropical air that Sara thought she would never tire of. Danny skipped along beside her, and Shane and Reagan were ahead of them with their heads together. Whatever they were talking about claimed their full attention. Every once in a while, she saw one or both of them in profile smiling at the other.

Sara thought back to the conversation she and Reagan had up in the room. Sara couldn't hide her annoyance. "So, which brother do you have your eye on?"

Reagan's eyes grew wide. "Whoa! Who says I'm interested in either one of them?"

"Oh, Reagan, I'm not a child," Sara retorted. She stepped out of Reagan's clothes and took the other set out of her suitcase. "Here," she said, gathering them up and handing them to her sister. "I'm done with these."

Reagan took the clothes and shoved them in a drawer. "Which one are *you* interested in?"

Sara aimed her sharpest look at her sister. "Neither. One." She rifled through her suitcase, found a tank top and shorts, and headed for the bathroom.

As she closed the door, Reagan shouted, "Dane's not married to me or anyone else, and he and I are just good friends. He's completely available and you can hear all about it from him."

Sara leaned against the coolness of the bathroom door and blew out a breath. *Dane isn't married? Maybe it was all a big misunderstanding.* She closed her eyes and the memories of that morning filled her mind. Sara replayed every smile, every look, and especially the feel of his hand in hers, and how safe and cherished she had felt in his arms, even though she'd literally just met him. There was definitely something very powerful between them. *Please, God,* she prayed. *Could you help fix this?* A sliver of hope blossomed in her chest.

Danny's voice brought her back to the present. "Miss Sara, look!" He ran up to her with three shells. "Feel how smooth this one is!"

Sara ran her finger along it. "Wow, that's awesome. Which shell do you like best?" She smiled as he chattered about each shell's best points. Then he announced that he liked them all the same.

Sara sighed. Even if he was single, Dane was a package deal, and Danny was adorable. But Sara lived in Wisconsin and they lived in Miami. It was ridiculous to even think about it. They couldn't even date. It felt like her life had fallen apart in the last three days, and she had no idea how to put it back together. The Disney deal was dead in the water. She didn't really want to go back to Chicago with Brandon and Morgan and their family, but at least she could be useful there. The prospect of going back to school in Michigan held no appeal now, either.

Sara looked out over the endless ocean, and the important lessons she learned since childhood filled her mind. Lessons about faith and trust. *Help me, Lord,* she prayed.

They walked a little further, and Danny wanted to stop to make a sand castle. "It's too bad we didn't have any pails or shovels to bring along," Reagan said.

Shane was on his hands and knees, scooping out big handfuls of sand, and Danny imitated him. "We don't need anything but our bare hands, right, buddy?"

"Right, Unca Shane." Danny was concentrating so hard, his eyebrows furrowed together and his little tongue peeked out of his mouth. He was adorable.

Sara and Reagan got down on the sand with them and twenty minutes later, they had an awesome castle to be proud of. "Let's get a picture," Shane said. He took his phone out and they took care of that.

"Where's Daddy?" Danny whined. "He said he was coming."

"I don't know, maybe he got tied up with work," Shane said. He pointed out toward the northwest. "Looks like a storm might be brewing." At that exact moment, his phone pinged with a text, and he read it. He looked at Sara and Reagan. "He said he'll meet us for lunch in thirty minutes. He hit a snag and he'll tell us about it then."

They took more pictures of Danny with the sand castle and assured him that they'd show them to Daddy. Then they began the walk back. Danny wanted to jog, and he and Shane went ahead. Sara and Reagan fell into step together.

Sara nudged her sister. "Looks like you and Shane are getting cozy."

Reagan looked up at her with hopeful eyes. "We'll see. You know I'm not good at relationships."

"Why do you think that is?"

Reagan didn't say anything for several seconds. "I built walls around myself after the debacle with Paul. It was just easier."

Sara couldn't believe it. "Reagan! That was ten years ago. Are you not over him yet?"

"Oh no, I'm completely over him." She shrugged. "I guess I haven't met anyone since who was worth taking a chance on."

"Not even Dane?" Sara wanted to kick herself the moment the words popped out.

Reagan smiled. "No, Dane isn't the one for me. For one thing, he's too young. But that's not really it. I'm too independent for Dane. He's a protector. The right woman will be his partner, but he'll still have that instinct, and she'll embrace it." Her gaze was earnest. "Think about it, Sara."

Sara was so confused, and didn't want to think about any of that right now. "And you think Shane is worth taking a chance on?"

Sara recognized that fierce determination in her sister's eyes, usually reserved for one of her news stories. "Oh yeah, I sure do."

36

DANE

DANE WAITED ON the beach near the path leading up to the patio for the others to get back. He'd gotten his shower and a change of clothes, and felt much better. He thought he'd be leaving St. Jardin later today, but now that plan was nixed. Maybe it was for the best. He'd just heard some folks in the lobby saying that a storm might be moving in. Dane paced nervously. He'd texted Shane about the snag he'd hit, and also asked him to somehow get Reagan and Danny away from Sara so he could talk with her alone.

He knew now that it would never work between him and Reagan, and he also didn't think he'd ever wanted it to. First, there was the age difference, which wasn't a deal breaker by itself, but there were other things. Reagan was so strong-willed. She always needed a cause, and Dane was more quiet and content to stay behind the scenes. He was a nurturer, and needed a woman who needed him.

And his brother needed a woman *exactly* like Reagan by his side in ministry. Dane shook his head to himself. *Wouldn't that be something?*

He paced back and forth. How could he convince Sara to give him another chance? He looked toward the direction he knew they'd be coming from, and pretty soon, he saw them, talking and laughing. Sara looked beautiful in a simple blue tank top and white shorts, and her golden hair shone in the sun. Danny rode on Shane's shoulders, and shouted when he saw his dad. "Daddy! We made a sand castle!" Shane lifted him off and set him on the sand, and Danny ran the rest of the way.

Dane ruffled his hair. "I'm sorry I got stuck working, buddy. I'm all done, though. We can play together all afternoon, but it looks like it might rain, so we'll figure something fun to do inside."

"Are we gonna have lunch now? I'm hungry!" Danny exclaimed.

Dane exchanged a look with his brother.

"Yes, we are," Shane said. "Let's go up to the patio and get a table." He held his hand out to Danny. "You can choose." In one smooth move, Shane's eyes connected with Reagan's, and she fell into step with him.

When Dane sensed that Sara was about to follow them, he stepped into her path. His heart began to beat faster. "Sara, please, could we talk?"

Her cheeks turned pink, and she had trouble meeting his eyes. "Um, sure," she said in a voice so soft, he could barely hear her.

He took a deep breath. "I'm so sorry about the misunderstanding. I didn't mean to hurt you. The ring was for show only." Her dark brown eyes were bottomless pools, and he felt terrible for any pain he'd caused her. "I'd really like to start over." He stuck his hand out and gave her what he hoped was his most engaging smile. "Hi, I'm Dane Corsica. Pleased to meet you."

She looked relieved and put her hand in his and giggled. "Hi, I'm Sara St. Clair. I'm pleased to meet you, too."

Dane took both of her hands then, and the zinging returned. "I—ah—I'm a Florida native, I work for the DEA, and I'm a single dad to an amazing little boy named Danny." Her smile got bigger. Dane swallowed. "Technically, I'm a widower, but we hadn't been together for a long time before that, um, happened." A sympathetic shadow crossed over Sara's features, and she squeezed his hands. He looked at her solemnly. "Someday soon, I'll tell you everything about that, I promise." He took a breath. "I'll be twenty-eight on June 20, and I love long, romantic walks on the beach." Sara threw back her head and laughed, and Dane joined her. "Okay, now it's your turn."

"I'm from Baraboo, Wisconsin. I was a vocal performance major for two years at the University of Michigan, and left there a year ago to help my brother take care of my two little nieces. Family is *everything* to me." Dane nodded his agreement. "But he's remarried now, and I'm…not sure what I'm doing. I'm—well, I'm at a crossroads in my life," she said. "I'm just waiting for God to show me, I guess." Dane rubbed his thumb over her knuckles. "I'll be twenty-two on July 7." Her perfectly-shaped eyebrows knit together. "Is that—am I too young?" Her voice trailed off.

Dane shook his head. "No, it's perfect," he said softly.

"Oh, good," she said, and let out a nervous breath. "And I love long, romantic walks on the beach, too—well, at least the one from this morning. That was my first." Her face flushed pink again.

Dane smiled. "I hope it's the first of many to come," he murmured. His heart swelled when she squeezed his hands and nodded. "But for now, will you be my date for lunch?"

She giggled. "Yes, but my stomach is fluttering so much, I don't know if I'll be able to eat much."

"Me, too," Dane replied. He took a breath, stepped a little closer, and moved his hands down to clasp her waist. A thrill shot through him when she wrapped her arms around him and looked up at him. "Sara," he said softly. He stared into her beautiful eyes. "I was married for almost six years and we weren't together most of it, but I never broke my vows." He paused. "I just—I would never do that."

"I know, Dane."

He tilted his head at her? "How? You don't even know me."

She nodded her head slowly. "But I do. My heart knows that you're a good man."

Dane felt the breath leave him. He drew her to his chest and wrapped his arms around her. After a moment, he released her and took her hand. "You ready?"

Her eyes shone with a promise of good days to come. "Yes."

37

SARA

SARA COULDN'T BELIEVE it. She wanted to pinch herself. *I must be dreaming.* She felt like she'd just come through a hurricane. Six hours ago, she'd been in captivity and was completely alone. Then she was rescued, reunited with her sister, and saw her summer plans go up in smoke. And then, in one pivotal moment, an amazing man opened his heart to her. Sara felt like she was walking on air.

She and Dane arrived at the patio, and she saw Reagan, Shane, and Danny at a round table in the far corner. Dane walked in front of her and wove through the tables. Her heart fluttered as she looked at their clasped hands.

Suddenly, a woman's voice came from their right. "Sara! Trey!"

Dane led her there and put his arm around her. "Cassie and Drew, hello."

How cool. That's his way of telling me their names. Sara easily slipped into her role and smiled at the couple. "Hi, Cassie, Drew. Nice to see you."

"What have you guys been up to?" Cassie asked.

Dane and Sara exchanged an amused look. "Oh, you know, just enjoying our honeymoon," Dane said. He pulled her a little closer, and Sara leaned into him, resisting the urge to sigh.

Sara felt Cassie studying her. "Sara, you look fantastic, much better than you did earlier in the week. Did you go to the spa day?"

"Yes, she did," Dane quickly answered. "She loved the seaweed wrap, didn't you, sweetheart?" His eyes sparkled at her.

Sweetheart. Sara nodded, never breaking her gaze with his. "Yes, yes, I did." She bit the inside of her cheek to keep from laughing.

"Have you been to the Queen's Garden yet?" Drew asked.

"Ah, no, we haven't made it there," Dane answered.

"Oh, you *have* to go. It's amazing!" Cassie exclaimed. "They're not doing a marriage ceremony there this week, but you can sign up for a tour."

In a flash, Sara's emotions went from panic to relief. That must be the symbolic marriage ceremony that Landon and Kelsea had participated in that had resulted in a legal marriage. Sara knew she wasn't ready for *that* step. She glanced at Dane and saw the same emotions flit across his features.

"We'll probably do that," Dane said. He took Sara's hand again. "We're joining our—ah, friends for lunch. Enjoy your afternoon."

"Bye," Sara said with a little wave, as Dane pulled her away.

"Bye," the couple echoed.

"Good job," Dane whispered. "You're a natural at this undercover stuff."

"Thanks," Sara giggled. "That was hilarious. Let's not tell Reagan the part where they said I looked so much better than I did earlier in the week!"

"Definitely not," Dane said with a laugh. They reached the table and Dane let go of her hand and put his arm around her, resting his hand lightly on her waist.

Shane and Reagan were sitting next to one another, and looked at them expectantly. "Hi, guys, how's everything?" Reagan asked brightly.

Dane looked at Sara, and their faces wore identical grins. "Great," Dane said.

"Yes, great," Sara echoed.

Shane and Reagan exchanged a glance. "Well, that's great!" Shane said with a grin of his own. Everyone laughed.

There was an empty seat next to Danny. "I want Miss Sara to sit by me!" Danny said. Dane held the chair out for her, and claimed the one on her other side. He scooted in, reached for Sara's hand under the table, and threaded his fingers through hers.

Sara met Reagan's gaze, and couldn't tell which of them was happier.

"Hello, everyone! May we join you?" It was Rose and Ike. Sara's gaze immediately went to Rose's feet, which were encased in pink Converse. The rest of her matching ensemble was pink as well. She and Ike were as cute as Kelsea said they were.

"Of course," the others replied in unison. There was plenty of room at the round table, and Shane and Dane fit two more chairs in. Sara picked up the menu. It looked like a regular restaurant menu, but there were no prices, since it was an all-inclusive resort.

Reagan's phone pinged, and she looked at it. "Oh, look, Sara!" she exclaimed and handed the phone over. "Here's our new nephew! Brandon and Morgan adopted a baby boy," she said to Shane.

"Oh, he's so adorable!" Sara exclaimed. She showed the picture to Dane and then passed the phone around.

"What did they name him?" Ike asked when the phone made it back to Sara.

Sara scrolled down. "Andrew James, for Morgan's dad and our dad." Her eyes grew wide. "AJ. They're calling him AJ." She handed the phone back to Reagan.

"That's the name April and Shelbie always wanted to call their little brother," Rose said.

"They came up with that before Brandon and Morgan even dated," Sara said in awe.

"Yes, back when they first met, when they couldn't stand the sight of one another!" Rose said, and everyone laughed.

The server came to get their drink orders. Once she had left, Rose looked at Shane. "What do you do, Shane?"

"I'm a pastor."

"Oh, that's nice," Ike said.

Dane raised his eyebrows. "He's *not* just a pastor." He told Rose and Ike about the Miracle Center, which of course they had heard of. Sara had, too. She couldn't believe Shane was its founder. They spent several minutes asking him all kinds of questions, and he seemed to always deflect the spotlight away from himself. Sara also noticed that her sister couldn't keep her eyes off him.

Their food arrived and everyone dug in. Dane remarked how much he and Reagan had enjoyed all the meals, which led to a long, fun story from Rose and Ike about how many mediocre chefs they'd suffered through before landing on their present outstanding one.

Shane spoke up. "Dane, you said you hit a snag with the case. Can you tell us anything about that?"

"Well, some. At first, the DEA said they wanted the— our witness back in Miami today. But our station chief is out of the country and can't interview him until Monday, and they'd rather he stay here, away from the media. He also said that I would have to be the one to bring him back." He looked at Sara. "They told me they would fly me home today and back on Sunday night, or I could stay here over the weekend if I wanted to, so I decided to stay."

Reagan's eyes narrowed. "Where's that *witness* now?"

Dane smiled at her. "That's DEA classified information, Ms. St. Clair. Don't worry, you'll get your exclusive when we get back to Miami on Monday."

Reagan glanced at Sara. "Actually, I'm flying home this evening. I need to get back to work." Sara resisted the urge to smile. *On a Thursday night?*

"Me, too," Shane said. "I have a full weekend coming up."

Dane slid a glance at Sara and winked. She swore she could hear his thoughts. *Yeah, they're about as subtle as a freight train.*

"What are your plans, Sara?" that question came from Rose. "You really should stay, too. After all, Trey and Sara Armstrong have reservations here through the weekend. The Carsons and some of the other couples and staff would wonder if you just disappeared. It would be so awkward for Trey."

Sara felt her face heating up. She took a breath and looked at Dane's beautiful, hopeful eyes, and knew the next words would change her life. "I could do that. I don't have anywhere to be."

"Good! That's settled," Rose said. She smiled at Danny. "Some of our staff have children who stay in our community room sometimes while they work. Danny can play with them."

"Cool!" he exclaimed, and smiled up at Sara. Her heart tripped.

One of the young men who worked the front desk came up to the table. "That storm we've been watching all morning is tracking south," he said, looking at the Goldmans. "The airport is closing in a couple of hours. I thought you'd want to know. The staff is already making preparations."

"Thank you, Luc," Rose said.

"Is it a hurricane?" Sara asked as the young man hurried off. Rose and Ike shook their heads. "No, these storms flare up and move through quickly this time of year," Ike said. "We thought this one was going to stay north of us. The airport will probably be open by tomorrow morning."

Rose looked at Shane and Reagan. "Looks like you'll have to stay with us another day," she said. "We had a last-minute cancellation for this week, so we have an extra room available."

Sara saw the brothers exchange a look. "Shane and Danny and I can stay there," Dane said. "Thanks so much Rose, Ike."

Rose stood. "It's no problem at all." She pulled at Ike's

arm, and he stood. "Well, since the weather has turned on us, we need to get busy and prepare for our Rain Dance night. It's *very* romantic." She looked around the table. "Not a *rain dance,* but just a dance to keep everyone occupied inside since it will be raining. This is what we do when it rains."

Ike seemed to have a deer-in-the-headlights look. "We do? I mean, yes, we do." He cleared his throat and nodded.

Rose took his hand and dragged him away. "Toodles! See you tonight at the dance!"

After they had gotten well away from the table, Sara giggled. "They're so cute! Just like Landon and Kelsea said."

Reagan rested her arms on the table. "I get the feeling Rose cooked all that up for our benefit. But I'm not going to any dance. I'll just go to bed early."

"I'm with you," Shane said. Then his face grew beet red. "I meant that I'm not going to the dance, either—not, ah, not the other part."

Dane grinned. "My brother has so many amazing gifts and abilities," he said to Reagan and Sara. "But dancing is definitely not one of them. Think bull in a china shop." They all laughed, Shane hardest of all.

Reagan's eyes lit up. "They have a game room with a pizza parlor." She shot Dane a mock frown. "We haven't been near it."

Shane's expression relaxed. "That sounds great."

Sara sighed. "I think the dance sounds wonderful," she said. Her heart skittered as Dane rested his arm along the back of her chair.

He slid a smile her way. "Hey, Danny, what do you want to do tonight?"

"Game room and pizza!" he exclaimed. All the adults laughed.

"How about you and Uncle Shane and Reagan do that, and I'll take Miss Sara out on a date?"

"What's a date, Daddy?" Danny asked.

Dane laughed. "It's when grown-ups who like each other a whole lot get dressed up and go somewhere together."

Danny seemed to mull that over. "Do you like Miss Sara a whole lot, Daddy?"

"I sure do." He looked at Sara with a gorgeous smile.

"Good. So do I, Daddy."

Dane leaned down and whispered in Sara's ear. "I can't wait to hold you tonight on the dance floor."

Sara began to tingle all over. She couldn't believe it, and her eyes connected with Reagan's. Even though a storm was coming, the hurricane had moved on, and left behind the beginnings of a whole new life for both of them.

The wind and rain arrived about an hour after lunch, so they spent the afternoon inside. The guys moved their things into their room, and agreed to meet in the game room.

When Sara and Reagan got there, they found Shane and Danny. "Dane had a phone call to make. He'll be here soon," Shane explained. When Dane got there, they all played Uno, and then Danny got out his Legos and other toys he had brought. Reagan and Shane left, and Sara and Dane sat on a couch by a window, watching the storm, holding hands, laughing, and talking. They were the only ones in the game room. Sara was sure all the honeymoon couples were in their own rooms.

"Hello, everyone!" In came Rose, wearing her usual bright smile.

Danny looked up from his playing. "Hi, Miss Rose!"

She looked at Dane. "I was hoping Danny could come and help us decorate in the dining hall. I could use a good helper."

Danny jumped up. "Could I, Daddy? Please, please?" Sara smiled. He was so cute and hard to resist.

"Sure, but you stay with Miss Rose and do everything she says."

Rose took Danny's hand. "I'm sure he'll be fine. I'll bring him to your room around 5:30, if that's okay."

"It's perfect. Thanks, Rose," Dane said.

After they left, Dane looked around. "We're alone," he said in a loud whisper. Sara thought his lopsided smile was adorable. He pointed at the spot right next to him and wiggled his eyebrows. He pointed to a footstool near her. "Bring that, too," he said.

Sara's heart began to pound, and she giggled as she scooted down next to him. His arms went around her, and they put their feet up. Sara thought this might just be the best moment of her life.

Dane rested his forehead against hers. "I'm so tired," he whispered, "and I need to take a nap or else I'm going to fall asleep on the dance floor tonight and really embarrass you."

Sara laughed. "Me, too. I don't think I slept at all last night."

"But I really, *really* need to kiss you before I fall asleep." Sara stared into his beautiful eyes, and everything went into slow motion. She lifted her lips to his, and his arms came around her. The kiss was soft and unhurried, with the promise of much more, when the time was right.

Dane slowly broke it off, and sighed. It was the most perfect first kiss Sara could imagine. She settled in and laid her head on his chest, and he pulled her close. She couldn't believe how utterly content she felt in his arms. Within minutes, she was asleep.

The next thing she knew, Dane's phone was ringing, and they both sat up and yawned. It was Shane, telling him that it was 5:30, and time to get ready for dinner.

Dane pulled Sara to her feet and they left the game room, hand in hand. His room was on the first floor, and he walked her to the stairway. "See you soon," he murmured, and pressed a quick kiss on her cheek.

Sara ran up the stairs, although she was sure her feet didn't touch the floor. When she got to her room, she went straight to the closet. She knew exactly what she was going to wear.

She heard her phone ping, and looked at it. It was fully charged now. She had several messages, but didn't want to take the time to read them all now. But one—*oh, no. This came just a couple of hours ago.* Sara swallowed and put it on speaker.

"Hi, Sara, this is Lance Petrie from Disney. I just had a call from a special agent at the DEA with a wild story about you being kidnapped. He assured me that you're okay and gave me a number in Miami to call to verify it." He paused. "I made that call, and I'm so sorry that you went through that. Listen, we'll hold your spot if you can get here first thing tomorrow. We'd still love to have you. Please let me know. Thanks, and take care."

Sara sat down on the bed in disbelief. *How in the world had Dane known who to call?* In the next breath, it became clear. He and/or Reagan had called Landon, who contacted Caitlyn. *He did that for me? What do I do now? I have a* third *chance to sing with Disney, but I've just met Dane, and don't want to jeopardize that.*

She showered, got dressed quickly, and put on her makeup. There was a tiny little vial in her makeup bag with a handwritten label on the top that said *Joy.* Reagan had given it to her earlier that day when she was packing. "It's one of those oil blends that Kelsea's always talking about," she'd said. "It's too flowery for me. But some of the other ones, I'm really starting to like." Sara opened the vial and took a deep breath. *Oh, that's wonderful,* she thought, and dabbed some on her pulse points and behind her ears. She hoped Dane would like it.

Then she sat on the bed and began to pray. And ten minutes later, she had peace. Sara knew exactly what she was going to do.

38

DANE

DANE ARRIVED AT Sara's door and straightened the lapels of his suit jacket. He couldn't believe how much had happened in this one short day. He had planned for their first kiss to happen at just the right romantic moment on the dance floor tonight, but once they'd been left alone this afternoon—thanks to Rose—Dane couldn't hold back one more minute. And he was glad he'd given in. Their first kiss had been perfect.

Deep in his heart, he knew Sara would probably be on a plane for Orlando in the morning, and he dreaded saying goodbye. But he felt that he needed to pave the way for her to follow her dream if she still wanted to. He'd prayed about it and deeply believed that it was the right thing to do. And if he had anything to say about it, the *goodbye* wouldn't be for long.

He knocked and the door opened, and there she was, a vision of beauty in an off-the-shoulder dress that floated halfway to the floor. The filmy layers were all the blues and teals of the ocean. His body ran cold, then hot. He stepped into the room and closed the door.

To his surprise, without saying a word, Sara stepped up to him, pulled his head down, and pressed her lips to his. Once Dane got over the shock, he wrapped his arms around her and kissed her back. Her lips were velvety smooth, and her hair was like silk in his fingers. Whatever her perfume was set his senses reeling, and she felt like heaven in his arms.

He wanted the kiss to go on and on, and it did.

When they finally came apart, he felt his face split wide open in a grin. "What was that for?" he murmured. "Whatever it was, I'll do it again, a thousand times."

Her eyes were shining. "You called Lance."

"I did."

"Why?"

He rubbed his hands on her arms. "I wanted him to know that you didn't just blow them off, that there was a valid reason that you didn't show up." He paused. *This was it.* "I wanted you to have the chance to still fulfill that dream if they would agree. They still want you. He made that very clear."

"And I want to go. It's been my dream. But now, there's only one thing that would keep me from it." She stared into his eyes. "You," she said softly.

That one word hit Dane with the force of a tornado. He had to make sure he'd heard her right. He swallowed. "Me?"

"Yes, you and Danny. I'd like to sing with Disney, just for the summer." She took a breath. "But if you won't wait for me, I'll come with you now."

Dane decided that sometimes, actions spoke louder than

words. He moved his hands up to gently bracket her face and kissed her, slow and sweet. He didn't know how each kiss could be better than the last, but it was.

Then he touched his forehead to hers. "I'll wait for you," he whispered. He raised his head and took her hands. "In fact, I have a lot of vacation time banked, and I'll get an extra week off after this case closes." He grinned at her. "Danny and I will be your groupies."

Sara laughed, a melodious sound that wove its way straight into Dane's heart. "I've never had groupies! I have a feeling this is going to be the *best* summer!" she exclaimed. Her beautiful eyes sparkled.

Dane couldn't resist. He leaned down and brushed his lips across hers. "Go ahead, call Lance now, and then we'll go on our first date." He lowered his voice. "By the way, you look *amazing*."

"So do you." Sara rubbed her fingers across the knot of his tie. "Very James Bond," she said with a flutter of eyelashes. "Save every dance for me tonight."

Dane kissed her again. "Count on it."

39

DANE

SARA LEFT ST. Jardin on one of the first flights out early that morning. Dane borrowed one of the resort's vehicles and took her to the airport. Their last kiss was filled with longing for the next time they'd see one another, in about a week. But they agreed that this was going to be a fantastic opportunity for Sara, and they'd get through it.

Memories from the night before filled Dane's mind. He felt that Rose and Ike had orchestrated the shimmering, romantic evening just for him and Sara.

Now, he helped load Shane's and Reagan's bags into Sadie-belle's trunk. Moni was delighted to be taking them to the airport.

"I like your car, Moni!" Danny exclaimed. "It's so cool!"

Shane murmured in Dane's ear, "You sure this thing will get us to there in one piece?"

Dane smirked. "Time to exercise those prayer muscles."

Shane laughed. "I'm working on a plan to get her a better vehicle," Dane said. "You know, to thank her for all her help."

Reagan was chatting with Moni, so Dane had a few moments of privacy with his brother. Shane nodded. "That's nice. How are you and Sara going to do the long distance thing, if it works out?" he asked.

"Well, I have a ton of vacation time banked, and I get an extra week off after this case closes. So—we'll see what happens. I have a couple of plans in mind."

Shane smiled. "I can see the wheels turning."

Dane felt a tug on his elbow, and turned. It was Reagan. "Excuse me," she said to Shane. "I need a few minutes with my good friend." They walked across the grass and stopped under a tree. Reagan looked up at him earnestly. "You break my sister's heart, Corsica, and you'll have me to deal with."

Dane smiled and nodded. "I have every intention of taking care of Sara's heart, and every other part of her, for a very long time."

"Good. Hold out your hand." Dane frowned and did as she asked, and she laid the engagement and wedding rings on his palm. "You may need these again someday."

Dane smiled, slipped the rings in his pocket and hiked a thumb over his shoulder. "And speaking of hearts, you be careful of his. He's waited a long time for the right woman. Remember, I told you to hold out for the best of the best. That's it, right there."

Reagan's eyes clouded over. "I'm not sure I'm the right woman, yet. I have some soul-searching to do, and I need to work on my relationships with my family." Then she smiled. "For now, I'm enjoying cultivating a friendship with him, and I *really* want to learn more about the Miracle Center. I'm fascinated by it."

Dane was certain she wanted to get in there and see how it all worked. "It's an amazing place." He began walking back to where Moni was waiting. "It wouldn't have worked between us, you know."

Reagan smiled. "I know. You're still one of the best friends I've ever had, and I hope that'll never change."

Dane pulled her to his side and squeezed. "You were a great partner, Reagan."

"Thanks."

When they reached Shane, Reagan punched Dane lightly on the arm. "Call me on Monday the minute I can do an interview with Rogers."

"Yes, ma'am," Dane barked with a salute. He and Shane laughed.

Reagan rolled her eyes at them. "After I get this story filed, I'm taking some vacation. I want to see Sara on the road and then go visit our brothers and get to know their families. And spend some time with Mom and Dad."

"Danny and I are going to all of her weekend shows," Dane said. "You can come with us sometime."

"We need to go," Shane said.

"Goodbye, Unca Shane and Miss Reagan," Danny said. He hugged his uncle, and Dane was surprised but touched when Reagan leaned down to give Danny a hug.

Shane grabbed a hold of Dane's hand and pulled him into a hug. "Our women pulled off the greatest bait and switch in history, didn't they?" he whispered in Dane's ear.

Our women. Dane laughed and nodded. "They sure did, brother. They sure did."

40

EARLY OCTOBER
MIAMI, FLORIDA

DANE

AFTER DANE ESCORTED Governor Rogers back to Miami, top leadership of the DEA took over, and Dane's involvement decreased dramatically. In exchange for the governor's testimony about Doug Navarro and others involved in the Cuban anti-cancer drug conspiracy, no charges would be filed against him. He was taking some personal time away to be with his family, and Dane had learned that he was considering resigning from office.

Reagan got her exclusive, and it catapulted her already successful career to the next level. She was able to pick and choose her assignments, and had backed way off on her hours. She had a new passion now, volunteering at the Miracle Center and spending time with Shane. They weren't officially dating, but Dane thought they may as well be.

The summer months were the best time of Dane's life. He and Danny made countless trips back and forth to Orlando, and it was worth every mile. They drove to other cities in Florida where Sara's group performed, and Dane loved making memories on the long car trips with his little son.

The first time he saw Sara on stage, he knew he was completely in love with her. Everything about who she was as a person came out when she was performing in front of a crowd, and the first time she sang solo, Dane almost fell out of his chair, her voice was so pure and beautiful. He was so proud when she introduced him as her boyfriend to her fellow performers.

Weekends were packed with performances, but the first time Sara was able to get a few weekdays off, she came to visit them in Miami, and Dane loved showing her where he had grown up. Nick and Julie Corsica were already wildly hopeful about the prospect of having Sara as a daughter-in-law. Dane hadn't brought it up, but his parents had, and he was thankful for their blessing, although he didn't want to rush things. He and Sara hadn't talked specifically about their future. They were just enjoying being in love and living in the moment.

Sara's contract with Disney went till the end of September. She could have opted out early in order to begin the fall semester, but she was still weighing her options and decided to wait. After her final concert, she and Dane decided to drive to Wisconsin on what Sara dubbed the *St. Clair Family Tour,* and Dane took Danny out of school to go with them. Their first stop was St. Louis to spend a weekend with Landon and Kelsea and the twins. Danny loved the little ones, and it cemented the desire in Dane's heart to give him brothers and sisters someday.

Dane enjoyed talking with Landon, and told him about

Moni's Gremlin and how he wanted to get a better car for her. They couldn't have pulled off Sara's rescue without everyone, but Moni was special. "Do you know anything about how to get a car onto the island, I mean, the legal hoops to jump through?" he asked Landon. "I was thinking of getting something in Miami and shipping it over from there. Maybe a good used VW bug. That seems to fit Moni."

Landon let out a moan. "Dane, you're the answer to my prayers." He grinned. "My wife has a VW bug from her single days that's obviously not a good mode of transportation for our growing family, but she's emotionally attached to it and won't let it go. She says it has to have *exactly* the right owner, someone who will love it as much as she does." He sighed. "It's in storage and I'm shelling out money every month for it. If you could take that off my hands, I'll be in your debt. I'll give you anything you ask for."

Dane bit his tongue. *Your younger sister's hand in marriage?* He really did hope that Landon would be his brother-in-law one day. He thought about Moni's affection for Sadie-belle and laughed. "Did Kelsea name the car?"

"Myrtle, as in Myrtle the Turtle," Landon said with a chuckle. "It's green."

"Moni will be the perfect owner, I assure you," Dane replied. "I hope she and Kelsea can meet the next time you go to St. Jardin." He knew the St. Clairs visited the resort at least once a year, usually for their wedding anniversary in January.

"I'm not sure when that'll happen, with more babies on the way, but we'll meet her someday," Landon said. "I'll check into the legal stuff and let you know. And I'll take care of getting Myrtle to Miami—well, once I convince Kelsea to agree."

"A nice piece of jewelry might grease the skids," Dane said.

Landon laughed. "Jewelry doesn't work on Kelsea," he said. "Now Sara—that's a different story. The bigger the bling, the better. Have you figured that out yet?"

Dane laughed in response. "Yeah, that was apparent pretty quickly. But thanks for the tip."

"Anytime," Landon said. "Happy to help you out, Dane. I mean that." Something in Landon's eyes told Dane that he had a real ally.

Their next stop was Chicago, at Morgan and Brandon's beautiful country home. Dane could hardly believe that it had been just a few months since he'd been there at their wedding, when he and Reagan were hiding out. It felt like he and Sara had been together forever.

It took about five minutes for Danny to become best friends with April and Shelbie. The three of them were inseparable and spent hours playing outdoors. Dane didn't feel that he knew Brandon very well compared to Landon, with whom he had spent a full day making arrangements for his and Reagan's escape to St. Jardin, and several phone calls when they were there. He felt like Sara and Brandon had a special bond, as Landon and Reagan did, and enjoyed spending time with Brandon and getting to know him.

Reagan was on her own "St. Clair" tour, but in reverse. She had started at their parents' in Wisconsin, and showed up at Brandon and Morgan's the evening before Dane, Sara, and Danny planned to leave, so they stayed an extra day. Dane felt completely comfortable with their friendship, and had a chance to bring her up to speed—off the record—with what had happened with Governor Rogers.

Sara spent a lot of time with both Brandon and Morgan, and held baby AJ at every opportunity. The first time Dane looked at her face when she held the baby, he realized more than ever that he wanted to build a life with her, have children with her, and grow old with her.

That made it easy to have *that conversation* with Jim and Janice St. Clair on their last night in Wisconsin, after a wonderful few days of getting acquainted and visiting some of the area's attractions, including Danny's favorite, a spectacular indoor water park. Fall was in all its glory now, and Dane had never seen the colors. That was one of his favorite parts of the trip.

Sara had gone to have coffee with her friend, Caitlyn, so it was the perfect opportunity to talk with her parents privately. With a full heart and great humility, Dane told them that he knew that Sara was the woman God had chosen for him, and they joyfully and tearfully gave him their blessing. He told them that he wanted to wait until Christmas or New Year's to propose to her, and they promised to hold his confidence until then.

He and Sara hadn't talked specifically about what would happen with their relationship now, and it was time to have that conversation. A couple of times, she'd said that she was still trying to make up her mind about going back to school, and Dane wanted to give her all the space she needed to make that decision.

But now, he was ready to take a big, important next step that might help her decide. He got Danny ready for bed, read to him and said prayers, and went to sit on the front porch to wait for her.

41

SARA

SARA AND CAITLYN hugged one more time. "Bye, boo, love you," Caitlyn said.

"Love you, too," Sara replied. They'd had such a wonderful time catching up. Caitlyn was so thrilled to hear everything about Sara's great time touring with Disney. She was anxious to meet Dane and Danny, and Sara promised her that would happen next time they came north. She *knew* there would be a next time.

She texted Dane when she left the coffee shop, and he was waiting on the porch when she pulled into her parents' driveway. Her heart swelled at the sight of his lopsided grin. Sara still couldn't believe that she could love someone so completely, so deeply, and feel that same love in return. She was ready to take the next step in their relationship, and couldn't wait to tell him her surprise.

He got up and trotted to the driveway, and opened her door when she turned the car off. Sara greeted him with a warm kiss, and he took her hand. "Go for a walk?"

"Of course," she said. "Hold on." She slipped her phone in her pocket, and put her wallet back in the car. They set off and turned left at the end of the drive. She knew exactly where they were going—where they'd gone every night since they'd been there—to the little gazebo overlooking a private lake that sat within the subdivision. They went to "their spot" and sat down. The stars were out in all their glory, and an almost-full moon shone down. The autumn breeze whispered across them like silk, carrying the scent of woodsmoke and leaves. Dane put his arm around her, and Sara snuggled in. She thought she could stay here for the next hundred years.

They sat there for several moments, and then Dane looked into her eyes. "I want to talk about the future, Sara. Our future." Her stomach began to flutter, and he took her hand. "For a long time, I wondered if I would be alone for the rest of my life to raise Danny." She could see his expression in the moonlight, and she'd never loved him more. "It's ironic, you know? I was reckless when I was young, but the biggest mistake of my life led to the biggest blessing of my life." His eyes teared up. "Danny brings me so much joy, every day." Sara squeezed his hand. "You and I haven't known each other that long, but I'm sure God sent you to me, and this summer—well, it's been the best time of my life."

Sara leaned up and kissed him. "Mine, too. I'm crazy about you and Danny."

"I want to get to know you even better. That's going to be hard from fifteen hundred miles away." Sara's heart began to beat faster as his chocolate brown eyes melted into hers.

"Now that I have Danny full-time, it's a much bigger decision. The most important thing is to provide stability for him. I'm not sure how to make a long-distance relationship work. Wisconsin or Michigan is a long way from Florida."

Sara nodded. "I completely agree," she said. She could hardly contain her excitement, and her hand inched toward her pocket. "Oh, Dane——"

He smiled and silenced her with a quick kiss. "I'm not finished yet."

"Okay," Sara said, willing her heart to slow down.

"So, like I said, making a long-distance relationship is hard work." He took a deep breath. "There's an opening in the Detroit field office, and also one in Milwaukee. The Milwaukee job is a better fit for my skill set, but if you decide to go back to Michigan, Danny and I will move there." He swallowed. "I love you so much, Sara."

For perhaps the first time in her life, Sara was at a loss for words. "You'd do that for me?" she whispered. "You'd leave Florida? Leave your parents and your brother, take Danny away from them? They're your support network."

Dane nodded. "Oh yeah, I would, sweetheart." He leaned in and kissed her tenderly, and she held him tight and kissed him back.

Her eyes were moist when they came apart. "I can't believe it, Dane." She pulled her phone out of her pocket and opened it. "I'm so happy that you're willing, but it's not necessary." His expression was anxious as she handed it to him.

His eyes scanned the e-mail that she'd received just this morning. "You're—you're *transferring* to Miami University?" His face was incredulous.

Sara bounced up and down with excitement. "Yes, I've been accepted! They have a top-notch early childhood education program, and they've agreed to apply most of my credits. That's what I want to do, Dane. I'll start in January, but I want to move to Miami now. Reagan said I could stay with her for a few months and see how it goes. I—I want to get to know my sister better, too." She couldn't tell what he was thinking.

Dane pulled her to her feet, lifted her up, and spun her around, his laughter mixed with hers. When he set her down, she put her hands on his shoulders and looked up at him.

"Thank you," he whispered, and covered her lips with his. He raised his head and smiled, his gorgeous brown eyes crinkling. "Now I don't have to learn how to live in the snow!"

42

SARA

"I REMEMBER THIS island!" Danny exclaimed as he looked out the window of the plane. They were on their final descent into St. Jardin. He looked up at Sara with big brown eyes. "I was just a little kid then." Sara smiled at Dane who was on her other side, and squeezed his hand.

This was Dane and Sara's first trip back to St. Jardin. In two days, they would marry on Christmas Day, and she would officially become Danny's mom. Her heart was so full, she thought it might burst.

They had a smooth landing and quickly got through customs and trundled all their baggage out to the curb.

"I'm heeeeeeeere!" A jolly voice exclaimed, and there was Moni with her trademark smile. She gave jubilant hugs to everyone. "I brought Myrtle the Turtle with me! I never can thank you enough!" she said as she laid both hands on the car and leaned in like she was hugging it.

Sara wondered how they were going to fit themselves

218

and all of their baggage into Myrtle, but Moni had already thought of that. Gustav was parked behind her in a four-door sedan that was in surprisingly good shape. Dane and Sara greeted him warmly. "I will bring all your luggage, and you can ride with Moni," he said.

"Oh goody! I get to ride in Myrtle!" Danny exclaimed.

The plan was to go straight to the Boogie Shack for lunch with Moni's family. All of them had been invited to the wedding, but Dane and Sara wanted a chance to visit with them first. And they had a special gift for Louie and his wife, Evie.

When Dane had gotten back to Miami after their trip to Wisconsin last year, he had received unexpected news of monumental proportions. His first wife and Danny's mother, Sally Ann, had never had much in the way of worldly goods, but Blayze, the international supermodel, left behind a fortune. Some of it was placed in a trust for Danny that he would inherit on his 25th birthday, but the bulk of it, she left solely to Dane. She had penned a poignant letter of apology to him that answered a lot of questions and helped him achieve closure regarding their marriage and the events that led to her downward spiral and eventually, her death. Sally Ann also said that she wanted her earthly fortune to make a real difference and provide a better life for people who needed it, and that she trusted Dane more than anyone else to make that happen.

Dane and Sara didn't want any of the wealth for themselves. Dane thought he would want to leave the DEA someday, but wasn't ready for that yet, and Sara was working hard to complete her college degree. They wanted to save to buy a house and add more children to their family once they were married. They had agreed to just park the money and not make any life-altering decisions. They were praying about the best ways to honor Sally Ann's wishes.

But one thing they had agreed that they wanted to do as soon as possible was to provide a better dwelling for Moni and her family. Landon had done all the legal legwork and today, Dane and Sara were about to reveal the plans for a project that would kick off in the coming year, and they were beside themselves with excitement.

When they entered the restaurant, the noisy group broke out into applause. Dane and Sara greeted everyone with hugs, even the ones whose names they couldn't remember. Then Evie and some of her children came out of the kitchen with a delicious lunch, and they all ate and laughed together.

After that, they brought out a large, beautiful cake and Dane and Sara cut it and fed it to each other. "You need practice for the real thing!" Moni exclaimed.

Dane looked at Sara, and she knew it was time to make their announcement. "Louie and Evie, it's time for you to sit down and relax," Sara said. They had both been bustling around getting food and drinks for everyone. Once the couple was settled with pieces of cake and something to drink, Sara went and stood by Dane.

"Sara and Danny and I are so happy to be here with all of you," Dane said as he looked around the room. "I'm not much at making speeches, but—well, I guess the simplest way to say it is that I received a pretty generous inheritance recently, and the person who left me the money only asked that I use it to help others to have a better life."

He turned to the parents of this most unlikely family.

"Louie and Evie, you've given your hearts and everything you own to make a family and give them a better life, and we'd like to help you with that." He walked over to Louie and handed him an envelope. "Here's a little something to start the year off right," he said.

Louie looked at Evie and back to Dane. He looked like he didn't know what to do. "Go ahead, open it," Sara said. She was so excited she would hardly stand it.

Louie pulled the back flap open and looked in the envelope. His eyes went wide, and he let out a sob. "Fifty—fifty thousand dollars? You're giving us a check for fifty thousand dollars?" Evie screamed and covered her face as the room erupted in pandemonium. Tears streamed down hers and Louie's faces, and they embraced.

Sara couldn't help it, and she began to cry. She looked at Dane and saw that he was tearing up, too. Louie and Evie stood and held out their arms, and drew Sara and Dane into them. "Thank you, thank you so much," they exclaimed.

When everyone had composed themselves, Dane held up his hand. "This is just the start," he said. "We've drawn up plans for a brand new home for your family, and I'll go over all that with Louie and Evie later." He looked at them affectionately. "So you can make it just the way you want it." Sara was so proud of Dane. He had put the whole plan together with his father, who owned a construction company. Because of the size of Sally Ann's estate, it had taken over a year for everything to move through the legal system. Landon was advising Dane and had put him in touch with a good attorney in Miami who was setting up a foundation, which Dane and Sara had decided to call *Sally Ann's Hope*.

As the room erupted in more cheers, Sara looped her arm

through Dane's and reached up to kiss his cheek. "I love you so much, Dane. I can't wait to be your wife."

"I can't believe that by this time tomorrow, we'll be married." Dane squeezed Sara's hand and stared into her eyes. It was the next morning, and they were walking along the shoreline just as they had on the morning they met.

"This is perfect, having the wedding here and having it all to ourselves," Sara said. The Goldmans had closed the resort for the entire week. She looked around worriedly. "But I won't relax until Reagan and Shane get here. What time is it?"

Dane put his arm around her. "About two minutes later than the last time you asked. Sweetheart, they'll be here. Shane texted that their flight left on time."

Sara's left hand rested on Dane's chest, and her spectacular princess-cut engagement ring sparkled in the sun. Dane had sold the bridal set Reagan wore when they were undercover so Sara could have something all her own. "I can't get married without my sister," Sara said. Rooming with Reagan had worked out great and brought them much closer. "And you can't get married without your brother," she added.

Dane stopped and locked his hands behind her waist. "They'll be here." He lowered his voice. "Can I help you get your mind off them?" He touched his lips to hers.

Sara smiled and gave herself over to his kiss. "Have I told you today how much I love you?" she said.

"Yes, but I never get tired of hearing it," Dane said. He took her hand and they walked up the hill and through the gardens to the resort's main building. They crossed the vacant lobby and entered the main dining room, where the rehearsal dinner was to be held that evening.

"Oh Dane, look!" Sara exclaimed. Both their parents and Sara's brothers and their wives were turning the room into a winter wonderland. "It's beautiful!"

"Here's the bride and groom!" Sara's dad shouted, and everyone stopped what they were doing to applaud.

Danny came skipping over to them with April and Shelbie. They had turned into the Three Musketeers. The smaller children, Rose and Isaac, AJ, and Landon and Kelsea's younger twins, Faith and Emma, were being kept under their mothers' and grandmothers' watchful eyes.

"Daddy! Mama Sara! Come look at what we're making!" He took their hands and dragged them over to a table where Morgan had all kinds of art supplies set out for them. Danny and the girls chattered excitedly about the decorations they were making for the reception tables.

"Morgan, this is great," Sara said.

"One of the perks of being an artist," Morgan said with a laugh. "I would have filled an entire suitcase with my 'art clutter,' as Bran calls it, if I could have talked him into paying the extra baggage fees."

Sara hugged Morgan. "How's he doing?" she whispered. Brandon was sitting at a table near the front of the room untangling miles of red and white lights being hung throughout the room by his and Dane's fathers.

Morgan sighed. "As usual, trying to overdo. Doctors make the worst patients."

"I'll go keep him company," Dane said, and set off in that direction.

"Thanks, Dane," Morgan called after him.

Sara studied her brother. "He looks better even since you got here yesterday." Brandon had been diagnosed with early-stage prostate cancer earlier that year and was undergoing a new treatment regimen.

Morgan nodded. "It's good to get him out of the Chicago winter," she said. "The sun and sea air have already done wonders for him." She sighed. "I wish I could just keep him here, but if I bring that up, he'll just feed me his 'I'm a city boy' line. He's itching to get back to work."

Sara looked at Morgan intently. "And how are *you* doing?"

Morgan's eyes welled up, and she swiped at them. "Fine. Of course I worry about him. I worry about everything."

"But his numbers are looking real good, and the doctors are optimistic, right?" Sara said. She squeezed Morgan's hands.

Morgan nodded. "Yes. They caught it early. But cancer is so scary." She closed her eyes. "I love him so much," she whispered. "I can't—"

Sara drew her sister-in-law into a hug. "I know." She drew back after a moment and blinked her tears away. "He's going to be fine, Morgan. In fifty years he'll still be driving you crazy."

Morgan gave a shaky laugh and wiped her eyes. "I'll take it," she said.

Kelsea came up on Morgan's other side, holding little AJ. Morgan held her arms out and he let out a squeal.

"Did you want to decorate the cake?" Kelsea asked her sister. "Mom and Janice offered to do it." Today was Brandon's birthday and they were going to celebrate tonight after the rehearsal dinner.

"They can do it," Morgan said. "You know what? On

second thought, I want to." She kissed her son's cheek. "You want to help Mommy decorate Daddy's cake?"

"Cake!" AJ squealed.

Suddenly, there was a commotion by the door, and Sara realized that Reagan and Shane had just arrived. "Reagan!" She cried, and ran to her sister. When they embraced, Sara whispered into her ear, "Your hair looks great!" Then she hugged Shane, and everyone else arrived to greet them. Sara moved out of the way to make room.

Her brothers were the first ones to bring it up. "Your braid! You cut off your braid?" they exclaimed. Reagan's dark brown hair was fashioned into a smooth, shoulder-length bob.

Reagan glowed. "It was time for a change."

"It looks fantastic, Reagan," Kelsea said.

Morgan nodded. "I'm not sure I would have recognized you if I hadn't known you were coming."

"You look years younger, Reagan," Dane called out.

Her eyes narrowed. "Watch it, Corsica," she said with a grin, and everyone laughed.

Dane whispered to Sara, "I'm glad Reagan has gotten over her phobia of hugging."

Sara smiled up at him. "It wasn't a phobia. She just isn't an affectionate person."

"Make that *wasn't*," Dane said. "I think my brother has done wonders for your sister."

"Him and God." Sara squeezed his hand and moved to stand by Reagan. She looped her arm through her sister's. "Ok, everyone, we have an announcement." She waited until everyone was quiet, and tried to look sad. "Reagan is *not* going to be my maid of honor."

No one said anything, and Sara took in their confused faces. Then she looked at her sister. "Right, Reagan?"

Reagan gave a curt nod. "Yes, that's right. I'm not going to be Sara's maid of honor." She paused. "But I *will* be her matron of honor." She held up her left hand that had a gold wedding ring. Shane held his up to reveal a matching band.

There was a moment of stunned silence, and then everyone started talking and laughing and hugging again. Reagan and Shane were embraced and congratulated by everyone.

"This is fantastic!" Kelsea cried. "And after tomorrow, you two girls will have the same last name again!"

Reagan smiled. "Actually, it *won't* be the same after tomorrow. I kept St. Clair."

Shane put his arm around his wife. "One of the many concessions I had to make to get her to marry me," he said. Everyone laughed, and Shane planted a kiss on the top of Reagan's head.

"When did you—where did you get married?" Landon asked.

"On Thanksgiving Day," Shane said. He and Reagan exchanged a loving glance. "We just—we love all of you, but it was something we wanted to do quietly. It was just the two of us and a pastor friend of mine, down at the beach with Dane and Sara as our witnesses."

Reagan's face shone. She looked around the group. "You all know that I wouldn't have been a very good traditional satin-and-lace bride." Everyone laughed.

Shane took Reagan's hand. "And after the ceremony, I had the privilege of re-baptizing Reagan in the ocean."

"That's wonderful, Reagan," her mother said, and the others nodded in agreement.

"Did you know about this, Mom and Dad?" Landon said.

Jim and Janice exchanged a look. "They called us about a week ago, but we promised to keep it to ourselves," Jim said. "They wanted to tell all of you in person."

"Peanut kept a secret all this time?" Brandon said with an incredulous look. His eyes were sparkling and Sara knew he was teasing.

"Where's your diamond ring, Auntie Reagan?" demanded little Shelbie. "My mommy and all the other ladies have one."

Morgan grimaced. "I'm sorry, Reagan. She's so inquisitive."

"It's okay." Reagan smiled at her niece. "I didn't want one." Sara noticed that her sister was looking at Dane.

Dane laughed. "When we were fake married, I got her a diamond, and she said the engagement ring wasn't her style."

"Saved me a bundle," Shane muttered with a smile. Reagan elbowed him, and he put his arms around her, and everyone laughed.

Dane drew Sara close. "I told her then that it was the *real Sara's* style, and I was right," he said. "I definitely got the right St. Clair sister."

Shane's eyebrows lifted. "So did I."

The long, oblong dining tables were arranged in a large square for the wedding rehearsal dinner in the main dining room. Dane and Sara had chosen this arrangement over separate round tables because they wanted everyone to be able to see everyone else.

The babies and children were being cared for by some of

Moni's sisters who were now working at the resort, in the next building. Their parents were looking forward to having a "date night" and a few hours' reprieve.

The tables were covered with white linen with beautiful red and white flowers and greenery. Silver and crystal sparkled in the candlelight, and sparkling white lights lent a magical atmosphere.

Rose and Ike stepped to the microphone. "Would everyone take their seats, please?" Ike said.

After everyone had located their place cards and gotten settled, Rose smiled at everyone. "We're so happy to have everyone here on the eve of Dane and Sara's wedding," she said, smiling at the couple. "We'd like to have a blessing before the meal is served. Pastor Shane, would you be willing to do that?" she said sweetly.

Shane stood and made his way to the mic. "Happy to," he said. "It's at the top of my job description, you know: *offer prayer at all events*." Everyone laughed.

After the delicious meal had been served and cleared, Landon took the microphone and carried it over to where Rose and Ike were seated.

"We have an announcement to make," Ike said. He reached out and squeezed his wife's hand. "I'll let Rosie do it, since she's the talker in the family." Everyone laughed.

Rose smiled at the assemblage. "As you know, Ike and I have owned this resort for about eight years. Some of you may not know that we lived in Brooklyn our whole lives until we won fifteen million dollars in the lottery and ended up here on beautiful St. Jardin, and bought this resort." Sara already knew this, as did Dane, and they enjoyed seeing amazement on his parents' and brother's faces.

Rose looked at Ike, and he took over. "We never had children, and didn't have any family in Brooklyn when we left. And now, all of you are our family." His voice wavered, and his eyes grew bright. He smiled and reached for Rose's hand again.

She spoke in a clear, loud voice. "God has given us more than we could ask or think! And I'm not talking about the money. I'm talking about all of you dear people whom we have grown to love. Jim and Janice, and your four wonderful children." Her gaze turned to Kelsea and Morgan's mother, and the Corsica parents. "Beth, you and your two beautiful daughters, and Nick and Julie, whose wonderful sons are now forming new families with the St. Clair sisters—now that they've all figured out who belongs with whom—with a little help." Everyone burst into laughter.

Rose looked at Ike and took a breath. "I think most of you know that we were planning to turn the honeymoon resort into a family resort, but after conducting some feasibility studies, it's become clear that we can support both, so we're going to add the family resort. But we're not getting any younger, and this business is growing. We've decided to turn the reins over to someone younger who can devote the time and energy to carry this dream forward. So, to help that happen, we've put everything into a trust, and effective March first, the new owner/managers of the St. Jardin Honeymoon and Family Resort will be—" she paused.

"Landon and Kelsea St. Clair."

It felt like all the oxygen left the room, and then everyone began to talk at once. Many questions arose out of the chatter, and once it died down, Landon stood and walked behind Rose and Ike. He placed a hand on each of their shoulders.

"To answer everyone's main question, yes, we're moving our family to St. Jardin. This was a decision made with a lot of prayer and planning." His gaze connected with his wife's. "We think it will be a great place for our children to grow up." He looked around the room. "Of course, the down side is that we'll be farther away from all of you."

"So you'll just have to come and visit!" Kelsea called out.

"Well, if you insist!" Jim St. Clair said. Everyone laughed. "Will you be giving up your law practice?" he asked his older son.

Landon nodded. "I'll sell my equity in JJS," he said, referring to the law firm where he was a partner. "I'm ready for a change, and since St. Jardin is a trade partner with the US, I'll still be able to keep my law license and maintain my skills through all of the administrative and legal tasks associated with owning a business here."

"What kinds of things do you have planned for the combined resorts?" Brandon asked. "I assume you'll be adding more services."

Landon nodded, and looked at Kelsea again before turning his attention back to Brandon. "I'm glad you asked, bro," he said with a smile. "First off, we'd like to add on-site medical services. What's available on the island isn't really adequate for what we need." He paused. "You wouldn't happen to know a doctor who'd be willing to relocate here and take charge of that, would you?"

Silence hung over the group. Brandon looked at Morgan and took her hand. As close as her brothers were, Sara suspected that this wasn't the first that Brandon was hearing of it. "I might," he said with an enigmatic smile. Morgan's eyes filled and she laid her head on his shoulder.

Landon looked around the group. "Kelsea and I have talked about all sorts of other things we'd like to do." He looked at Morgan. "An art gallery, and an arts and crafts center for all ages." His gaze then moved to his younger sister. "A daycare/preschool for our staff children with programs for the children at the family resort."

Kelsea looked at Beth, who had just retired after a long career as an elementary educator. "There'll be a place for you, too, Mom, whenever you want to come. And Jim and Janice."

Beth's face brightened. "I'll sacrifice the northern Illinois winters for starters," she said.

"Hear, hear!" Jim said. Everyone laughed.

"I'm not ready to retire yet," Nick Corsica said. "But I'd love to talk about partnering with Corsica Construction when you're ready to start building. It will be easy to manage projects between here and Miami." He looked at his wife. "We'll give you the family discount," he said with a smile, and everyone laughed.

"That's fantastic, Nick, thanks." Landon turned his attention to Dane. "I'm not sure what we can come up with to rival the excitement of the DEA."

Dane held up both hands. "I've had enough excitement," he said, and put his arm around Sara. "Actually, I've been thinking about leaving. I'm ready for a new challenge. As soon as my wife graduates, we'll talk about it." Sara's heart skittered at the possibilities.

Landon gestured to Shane and Reagan. "Maybe you

could open a branch of the Miracle Center here, and of course, a newspaper."

Reagan laughed and shook her head. "I'm still doing some freelance writing, but that's it. For now, anyway." She looked at her husband. "My place is by Shane's side in ministry."

Brandon looked at her incredulously. "Words I thought I'd never hear out of you!" The group laughed. His gaze softened. "Sis, that's fantastic."

Reagan reached for Shane's hand. "I guess this is as good a time as any to let you all know that…this family will be growing."

Once again, there was a beat of stunned silence, and then the room erupted with noise and cheers.

Shane grinned and held up three fingers.

"Triplets? You're having triplets?" Sara shrieked, and the room got even noisier.

Reagan shook her head back and forth. She was laughing so hard, she could hardly speak. "No—I'm not—" She looked at her husband. "Shane, you have to explain."

"All right." Shane let out a breath. His smiling face turned serious, and everyone got quiet. "A couple in my—our—church, that I've known for years, was killed in a small plane crash about six months ago." Silence dropped down on the room. "We—we've started proceedings to adopt their three sons." He reached for Reagan's hand. "They're terrific boys. They're—eleven, nine, and six. We're so honored that God has chosen us to be their—parents." He choked up on the last word.

Landon squeezed the bridge of his nose. "Wow," he said. "This just keeps getting better and better. Shane and Reagan, that's fantastic." He looked at Sara and Dane. "You two are about to enter into the most sacred relationship that God created." He held out his hand to Kelsea, and she came to his side and their arms went around one another. "Almost six years ago, Kelsea and I were about to be married—to other people—and we both got jilted at the last minute. That heartbreak led to us meeting, in a most unlikely way, right here on St. Jardin." He looked at Rose and Ike tenderly and smiled, and then moved his arm in a wide arc across the room. "And look what happened because of a little matchmaking!"

"I'm still willing to serve as the island's matchmaker!" Rose exclaimed, and everyone laughed and cheered.

Landon looked at the clock. "It's getting late. Let's go get the little ones and meet back here for dessert." He looked at his brother. "It's time for a birthday party."

43

REAGAN

REAGAN WALKED OVER to where her parents were sitting. She'd wanted to have this conversation with them for the past year and a half, but her heart wasn't ready yet. She knew that now was the time. "Mom, Dad, could we talk for a few moments, privately?"

"Of course, Reagan," her mother said. They rose and followed her out a side door and through a garden to a couple of benches set at right angles. Jim and Janice sat down at one, Reagan at the other.

"I—whew," Reagan blew out a breath. "This is harder than I expected." *You can do this.* "Mom and Dad, I want to ask your forgiveness for all the things I've done over the years. I know I was such a big disappointment to you—"

"What are you talking about, Reagan Joy? You've never been a disappointment to us!" Janice exclaimed. She and Jim wore twin expressions of confusion.

Reagan's eyes filled with tears, and she swiped at them. "Oh, I know I was. All my drama in high school. Leaving the youth group and the church, and not following the path you wanted for me—"

Her parents frowned at one another. "All we've ever wanted for you was to be happy, Reagan," Jim said. He took her hand. "You had to find that path on your own. No one could choose it for you."

"More than anything, Reagan, we wanted you to have a right relationship with God, whatever that meant to you." Janice said. She scooted to sit next to Reagan and put her arm around her. "We made that vow to Him when we had you dedicated as a baby. We've prayed that for you every day of your life." Her eyes welled up. "And we're so glad that you've found your way back to Him."

Reagan fell into her mother's arms, overcome with tears. "But—I was so stubborn, so headstrong," she hiccupped.

To her surprise, her parents laughed. "Oh, you sure were!" Janice said, wiping her own eyes. "You burst into the world two weeks before your due date, after only four hours of labor." She smiled at Jim and looked back at Reagan. "When we took our first look at you, we knew that you were going to live life on your own terms."

"They called it *strong-willed* back then," Jim added.

"But the boys weren't strong-willed," Reagan said. "They were perfect all the time and did everything you wanted them to."

That elicited a huge laugh from both of her parents. "Oh, they certainly did not!" Janice exclaimed. "I'll admit, they were more compliant than you, but they weren't perfect."

Jim moved to sit on Reagan's other side. "Honey, God gave you your temperament and your strong will. We just tried to shape that and channel it in a positive way so that you would do great things in the world."

"And you have, and still are," Janice said, and kissed Reagan's temple. "We're so proud of you, Reagan, and always have been." She ran her hand over her daughter's hair. "We couldn't be happier for you. We know you're going to be a wonderful wife for Shane, and a wonderful mother to those boys."

Tears ran down Reagan's cheeks. She felt so safe and secure and *loved* in her parents' arms. "I love you both so much," she whispered. "But I still need to have your forgiveness. Please."

"Consider it given, Reagan," her dad said.

Her mom whispered, "of course, Reagan, we love you so much."

Reagan looked at them with new eyes. "Now I'm embarking on the biggest challenge of my life. I'm going to be a *mom.*" She felt her eyes filling up again. "I have no idea what to do. It's all happened so fast. I haven't had nine months to prepare."

Janice laughed. "Believe me, Reagan, it doesn't matter. This is one job that you can only learn *on the job*." Jim nodded his agreement.

Reagan looked between her parents. "Would you two— would you consider coming down after the boys move in? Maybe stay a few weeks or a month? And just tell me what to do?"

Jim laughed and put his arm around his daughter. He looked at Janice. "I think we can work something out. We'd love to spend some time getting to know our new grandsons, and our new son-in-law. But remember, you're not in this alone. Don't you think Shane should have something to say about it?"

"Oh!" Reagan covered her mouth and giggled. "I almost forgot!" All three of them laughed.

Suddenly, Shane came around the corner and stopped in front of them. "Hi, everyone. There you are, Reagan. I was wondering where you were," he said. "Forgot what?"

Reagan popped up and went to him, slipping under his arm and wrapping hers around his waist. "I forgot when it was the boys are moving in with us permanently," she said innocently. "Would it be okay if Mom and Dad came to visit after they've gotten settled in?"

"I think that's a fantastic idea. I think it will be around the first of February." He smiled warmly at his in-laws. "That's a great time to come to south Florida for an extended visit. Mom and Dad would enjoy that, too."

Janice shivered. "You don't have to invite me twice."

Jim stood, and Janice followed. "We'd like to pray for you two," he said. They came and wrapped their arms around the younger couple, praying that God would have His hand on the adoption proceedings, and everything would go smoothly, for His wisdom on Shane and Reagan as they prepared for parenthood, and His blessing on the new family.

When her dad said *Amen,* Reagan's heart felt completely at peace.

44

DANE

DANE LOOKED AROUND this group of incredible people that God had brought together. *What an amazing family.* His beautiful Sara was at his side, and Danny's little arms were wrapped around him. Dane's heart was full to overflowing.

Dane loved that the St. Clair family always had a big birthday celebration for Brandon on Christmas Eve, separate from Christmas Day, so he wouldn't feel cheated. Dane loved all of Sara's family, but had come to have a stronger bond with Brandon. It was obvious that he and his wife were deeply in love, that he was a man of great faith, and a devoted dad.

After all the gifts were opened and the cake and ice cream were consumed, Dane was surprised when Shane stood and cleared his throat. "Everyone, I'd like to lay hands on Brandon and pray for him. Would you all join me?"

Everyone gathered their children and they moved in close to form a circle around Brandon, who held little AJ on his lap. April and Shelbie stood on either side of him, and

Morgan stood behind him next to Shane, their hands on his shoulders. Dane was next to Sara, with Reagan on his other side.

Dane's eyes filled with tears as his brother prayed with eloquence and great faith on Brandon's behalf, and he heard others crying, too. He stood between Sara and Reagan, their arms wrapped around one another. When Shane finished his prayer, a hush settled over them.

Next to him, Dane felt Sara take a deep breath, and then her clear, angelic voice filled the room. *Praise God from Whom all blessings flow. Praise Him all creatures here below. Praise Him above ye heavenly hosts. Praise Father, Son, and Holy Ghost.*

Her *Amen* echoed through the room, carrying everyone's collective prayers heavenward. Dane blinked back tears. *Thank you so much, God, for this family.*

ABOUT THE AUTHOR

Writing is like breathing to Erin. Stories are running through her mind during most of her waking hours, and by the time she sits down at the computer, the words flow and time ceases to exist.

Erin was raised in Illinois and has lived in many places in the U.S., including on both coasts, but is a Midwest girl at heart. She spent many years as an educator from pre-school through college levels, and currently works in training and internal communications for a major global corporation.

When she's not writing, Erin loves spending time with her children and grandchildren, and playing in the garden (which equates to mostly pulling weeds) at her central Iowa home. Her secret indulgence is plain M&Ms.

Connect with Erin!

Email: ESQwrites@gmail.com
Website: www.ESQwrites.com
Facebook: Erin Stevenson Quint
Twitter: @ESQwrites

If you enjoyed meeting Landon and Kelsea St. Clair in *Bait and Switch*, read their story in *Plan B*, available in print and eBook.

***

PLAN B

Kelsea and Landon have each been left at the altar, and neither has a Plan B. They decide to escape to the romantic island resort where they've booked a honeymoon, to hunker down in solitude. Enter Rose, a spry, pink-haired matchmaker, and watch the fun begin.

If you enjoyed meeting Brandon and Morgan St. Clair in *Bait and Switch*, read their story in *Home to You*, available in print and eBook.

***

HOME TO YOU

Widower Brandon St. Clair is struggling to care for his young daughters while maintaining a high-pressure career. When he meets beautiful artist Morgan Anderson, their differences threaten to tear them apart. Can they find what they're both searching for and make a home together?